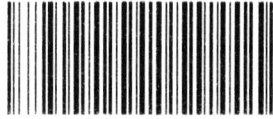

Man Of The House

Alistair McDonald

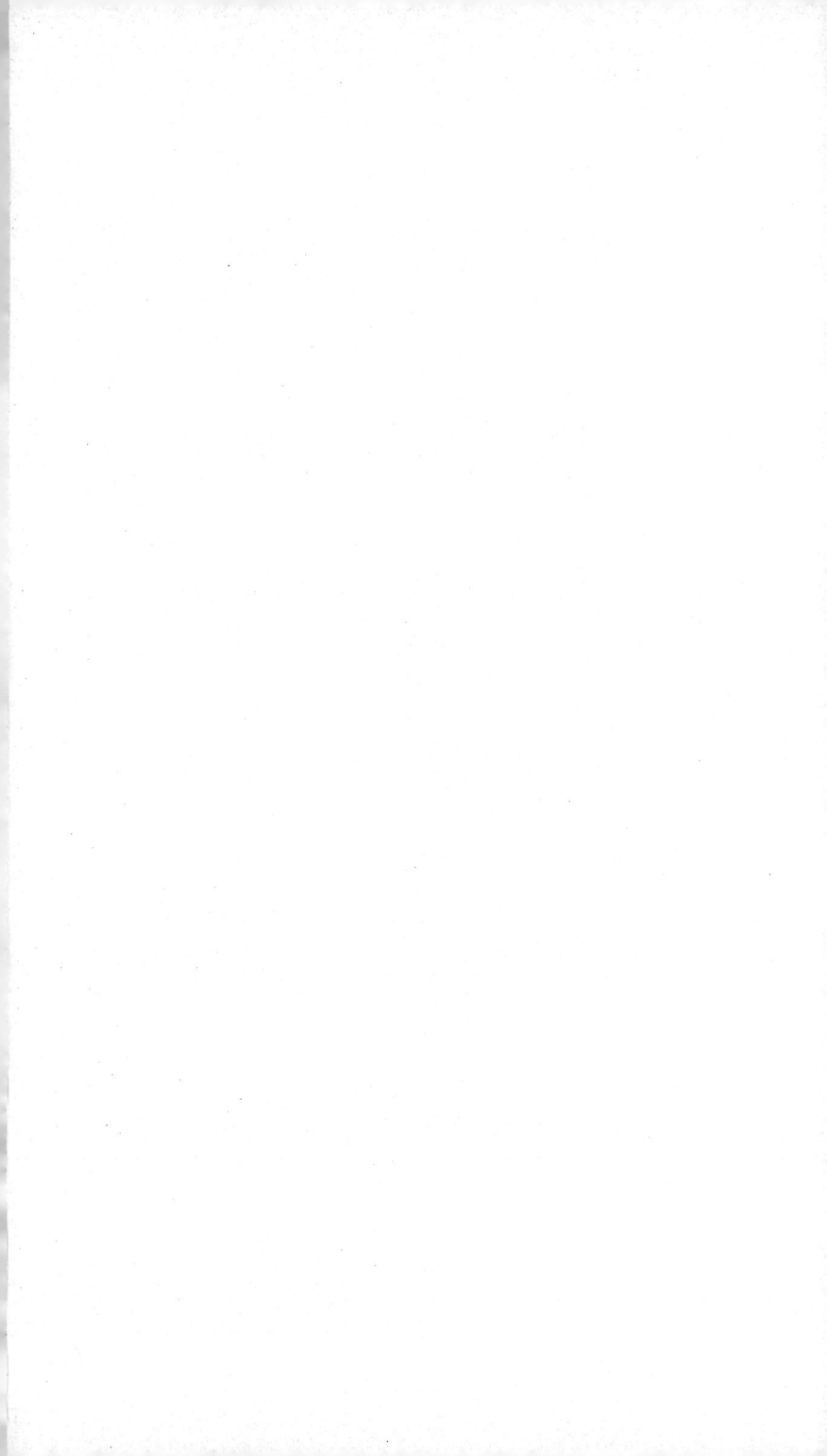

CONTENTS

CHAPTER 1

"David you better get going or you're going to miss the bus… again!" David heard his mother yell down the hall. Not again he thought to himself. He had missed the bus three times already this week and each time it meant missing his first period class and another tardy mark on his record. If he got a fourth this week let alone this month he would have after school detention. David grabbed his backpack and headed out the door. He watched his mother pull out of the driveway, and waved goodbye to her with one hand as he locked the door with the other. He turned around just in time to see the bus slow down and come to a stop. David took off at a dead run hoping the bus driver would wait just a couple seconds before driving off. He reached the bus just as the doors closed. Sally looked at him with a grin on her face as she opened the door.

"Almost missed it didn't you?" She smiled as David climbed on the bus. He just nodded as he passed her and

continued to an open seat. He relaxed into it as the bus continued to roll down the road towards the school. School was just another excuse to help get through the day. He knew his grades had been slipping for quite a while now. He used to be a straight A student, but now it seemed like he was struggling just to maintain a C average. The bus came to a stop in front of the school but David was in his own world. He exited the bus and walked towards the school. It was just going to be another day and the sooner he started the sooner it would be over.

That afternoon David was sitting in front of the school waiting on his sisters to arrive. Both Danni and Tina were in a different high school. Every day after school they would pick him up, and then the three of them would go home. It always bugged David that he had to go to a private school. It would have made his life easier to go to school with his sisters instead of riding the bus. David was starting to get impatient when the last bus left and most of the students had left for the day. Only a small handful of kids were left at the school and it was getting to be about four o'clock. His sister was never this late and he was starting to worry. He waited another 10 minutes then decided he was going to have to walk home. He climbed down off the wall he was sitting on and started down the sidewalk. He was looking at the ground and not really

paying attention to anyone or anything when a red car pulled up next to him.

"Sorry we are late." Danni said with little smile. Danni was the oldest at 17 and looked like their mother with long dark brown hair and green eyes. Tina was 16 and like David she had light brown hair and blue eyes just like their father. David was also 16 and liked to keep his hair cut short in a Caesar hairstyle. He felt it suited him well and most of the girls at school liked it too.

"It's ok I figured you just forgot about me." David replied in a low hurtful voice as he continued to walk down the sidewalk.

"Don't be so dramatic and get in the car." Tina said as she opened the back door. David stopped and turned to look at them both.

"It's ok I said, just go." David retorted emphasizing his words, as he turned and continued on his walk. Danni pulled the car up next to him again and Tina jumped out and grabbed him by the arm. Then Tina pushed him into the back seat and jumped in next to him. In a move that probably would have looked like an abduction to anyone else.

"Fine I'll ride in the back seat with you then. And quit being such a gloomy Gus." Tina replied falling against him as Danni drove away down the road. Tina's hair was cut

short but it still tickled David's cheek when she laid her head on his shoulder. "So what has you all bummed out little bro?" she asked. David turned to look at her but didn't say anything he was trying hard to keep the hurt look on his face. Tina just looked at him with puppy dog eyes and waited him out. She knew it wouldn't take long. David sat there silently trying to hold his own with her he knew it was useless he never could win with either of his sisters or his mother for that matter. He knew he was going to be the first to break.

David looked down quickly so that he wasn't looking Tina in the eyes any longer. He knew that would give him a few minutes more, but it was a lost cause. His eyes stopped when he got to his sisters sweater it was a button up light blue V-cut sweater. He could clearly see his sisters breasts stuffed into her matching colored bra with a little bow in the middle. The top button on the sweater was undone and he was trying to figure out if it popped open on its own or if his sister wanted it that way. He was mesmerized by the two creamy white breasts pushing to break free from their prison. He felt his sister put her hand under his chin and pull his head up so he was looking her in the eyes again.

"So what's wrong?" Tina asked again as she noticed her brother start to blush. David opened his mouth to speak

but no words came out. Tina just smiled and said "I guess you're just having a bad day." Then she turned her gaze out the window and laid her head on David shoulder again. David just sat there in silence trying to fight the urge to look down his sister's shirt again. But the temptation was just too great. He kept stealing glances the entire ride home. Occasionally his sister would look at him and then just go back to what she was doing. He wasn't sure if she knew what he was looking at or not, but he really didn't care either way.

As soon as they got home David headed to his room to start his homework. His sister Danni quickly changed and headed to her job at the local Dollar Store. Tina went to her room and was probably doing her homework as well. It was a routine they had fallen into fairly quickly after moving to this new house. David didn't care too much he liked having some structure to his life, and lately it seemed like that was one thing they hadn't had for quite a while. The phone rang startling David nearly making him jump clean out of his chair.

"I got it!" Tina said as she passed by his bedroom door. He heard her answer the phone but couldn't make out the conversation. He wasn't really interested in who or what it was about any way. He opened up his math book on the desk and started going over the Calculus problems that

were assigned for the day. It was only ten problems but it always took at least a half hour to complete them all. Luckily he had the chance to work on them in class, so half were already done. He was so engrossed in the work in front of him that he hadn't heard his sister hang up the phone or come back down the hall.

"Whatcha working on D?" she said as she walked up behind him. David nearly jumped out of his chair again. Tina leaned over and put her arms around David's neck and gave him a little hug. Tina had called him D for as long as he could remember it was kind of like her personal nickname for him.

"Just some math," David replied "Who was on the phone?" he continued.

"Just Mom, She is going to work late again tonight. She said we could order a pizza or something. What sounds good to you?" Tina said without moving her head from over his shoulder. She was still hugging him from behind but let go as he turned to face her.

"How you feel about Chinese? I don't feel like pizza tonight." David said

"That works for me" Tina replied then turned around and walked out the door. David could hear her in the kitchen ordering dinner for the two of them and having it charged to their mothers account. When his mother had

to go back to work she had set up charge accounts at a few of the local restaurants in town that delivered. It made it easier when she wouldn't be home to make dinner. Even though he and his sisters could both cook quite well it was always a nice treat. David continued to work on his math homework. This time he heard his sister approaching, but didn't say anything. Tina wrapped her arms around his neck again giving him another hug. This time David didn't jump he just continued to work on his final problem. She put her head down to the right of his and he could feel her breath on his ear.

"Dinner will be here in about forty five minutes. Oh and that should be a five not a six." She said as she pointed to the problem. David just erased the error and corrected it. David and Tina had always been close. So much so that people often thought they were twins. Tina though was actually eleven months older than David.

He liked it when his sister hugged him it always felt warm and safe. He honestly didn't really care that much about the hugs until after his Dad had died unexpectedly then it seemed like he and Tina had become much closer.

David had just turned 15 two days before his father had died. He remembered the day like it was yesterday. It was the day that his whole world changed. He was at home

getting ready for the camping trip him and his father were going on as part of his birthday present. It was about five thirty and his father had not gotten home from work yet. David had gone into the basement to get a few other items when he heard the doorbell ring. He heard his mother answer the door but couldn't make out the words that were being said. David walked up the stairs and saw a police officer standing just inside the front door. His mother had a look of shock on her face but she wasn't crying. Both his sisters were sitting on the couch crying and holding each other.

David's mother just turned and looked at him it was all just surreal. She hugged him tight as she told him that his father had been in an accident. The car he was driving was hit by another vehicle and was sent off the road. It hit the concrete barrier and rolled several times. His father had been ejected and the car rolled over the top of him. His father had died alone on the side of the road from the injuries he had sustained. Everything from that point was a blur. A few days later they had the funeral and then with all the bills his mother had no choice but to sell the house and buy a smaller one. They moved to a different town and he had to move to another school.

Shortly after that was when the nightmares set in. David could not sleep more than a few hours without

having one and it usually ended with him waking up screaming. His mother and sisters would do everything they could to calm him down and eventually he would fall asleep only to repeat the process an hour or two later. He remembered over hearing his mother explain to his teacher one day what had happened. The teacher just replied that no child should have to go through that. As the nightmares got worse and more frequent it seemed nothing was going to help. Eventually either over time or from sheer exhaustion the nightmares subsided.

Through all of this it seemed he took the death of his father harder than his sisters had. That and having to move to a new house and school just made things that much harder. His sister was always there through everything right by his side. Even after his mother had to go back to work she was there to take care of David. He had often thought that she was better at it than his mother was at times. But then he also knew that losing his father was really tough on his mother as well. He often heard his mother crying at night in her bedroom after she thought the kids had gone to sleep.

That was almost a year ago and it was still bothering him. His mom was working forty to sixty hour work weeks just to keep everything going smooth and Danni was working just to help take some stress off their mother.

David was fully aware that his grades were slipping at school and he knew why. He just didn't feel the purpose to try anymore. The school Psychiatrist said he just needed a little more time and they pulled him out of all his Advanced Placement classes. He knew that it had something to do with his father's death but he couldn't place his finger on the direct link. Without knowing that he just couldn't fix the problem. But all was not lost Science was the one class he wasn't struggling in. He and Danni had both been really good at Science. She had even gotten a scholarship to study at USC next year.

The doorbell rang and pulled David out of his memories. He got up from his desk and walked to the front door. Tommy Chang was the delivery boy standing on the other side of the door. His father owned Chu's Chinatown restaurant. They smiled at each other and Tommy handed him the bag of food. "Thank You" David said as he took it and handed Tommy a five dollar bill for a tip. Tommy just looked at it and his eyes got big. David knew that Tommy seldom got to keep his tips and worse was that he rarely got a paycheck from his father either. "Don't worry I won't tell your dad" David said as Tommy turned to leave.

At school David and Tommy were friends but after

school they never got to hang out because Tommy always had to be at the restaurant. One time Tommy got detention after school David recalled Tommy saying his dad was so upset he was grounded for a month. David told Tommy what was the point of grounding you, you don't have any social life anyway. Tommy just laughed and agreed. David watched Tommy ride down the street on his scooter and out of sight.

"Tina dinner is here." David yelled down the hall as he walked over to the table and set the bag down. He walked over and grabbed two plates and forks and set them on the table as he pulled the boxes out of the bag and opened them up. He divided the fried rice between the two plates and placed the empty box back in the bag. He did the same with the Sweet and Sour Pork and the Chow Mein. He placed one egg roll on each plate and then threw the containers into the garbage. He picked up his plate and placed it on the other end of the table. "It's going to get cold if you don't hurry up." David yelled down the hall again as he sat down.

He was staring down at his plate eating his food when Tina came out from her bedroom. She walked by the table and sat down in her chair directly across the table from David. David was lost in his own thoughts as he was eating his dinner. He hadn't even acknowledged his sister

when she sat down.

"So what do you think D, Do you like it?" Tina finally asked bringing David back to the real world. David looked up and almost spit his dinner out on the table. Tina was sitting at the table eating dinner just wearing her jeans and bra. David was stunned for a moment he tried to say something, anything but no words came out of his mouth he just sat there staring at his sister in awkward silence. Finally he looked back down at his plate. "Don't you like it?" Tina asked still smiling "You spent most of the car ride home looking at them, I just thought you would like to get a better look." She added. David looked up instantly from his plate with a look of embarrassment on his face. "It's ok D, that's what guys do. Don't worry about it, it's perfectly fine." Tina added as she took a bite of her Sweet and Sour Pork.

David sat there confused was he supposed to be looking at her face or her breasts. Crap what do I do now? He thought to himself. Before he could realize it he was sitting there just staring at that same blue bra she was wearing in the car. "Well it looks really nice sis." David finally managed to put a few words together. Swallowing hard he added "Aren't you cold?" Tina laughed and took another bite of her dinner. She was obviously enjoying watching him squirm, but for what purpose he didn't

know.

"This bra is a little small though I usually wear a 36D." Tina stated rather nonchalantly. David didn't know exactly what that meant but he figured it was why it looked like her breasts were going to explode out of her bra at any minute. "It was the last one they had in this style and color so I bought it anyway." Tina continued. David was trying and failing to look at anything but his sister's barely covered chest. It was a battle he was losing miserably. David put another bite of food in his mouth and chewed it slowly. "I can take it off if you want a better look at them." Tina said after a few moments then started to reach around her back to unfasten it.

"Uh...no that's ok." David replied swallowing hard again as he placed another bite in his mouth. Damn, why did I say no? He thought as he watched his sister move her hands back in front of her again and resume eating. He could tell she was enjoying her little game. It had to be a game he thought. Tina liked to play games and she loved to pick on him too. It was that type of relationship that all siblings went through he thought.

"Well let me know if you change your mind." She added with a little smile and resumed eating. David almost choked on the bite he had in his mouth, and just nodded. They sat in complete silence for what remained of their

meal together. David's gaze was fixated on Tina's breasts the entire time. He managed to look away a few times. But he always seemed to migrate back to looking at her ample bosom. One thing was for sure though; Tina was enjoying it just as much as David was.

David was finishing his homework in his room after dinner. He could hear his sister across the hall taking a shower. This house was definitely smaller than their old house. It only had three bedrooms which meant that his sisters had to share one room while he got the other one. To make matters worse their rooms had a shared closet that you could use to walk through to the other bedroom. It was more of a pain because his sister's clothes took up most of the closet space in both closets. Although the pass through ability was nice cause he could use it to sneak over to his sister's room at night. Sometimes he would use it and climb in bed with Danni if he was lonely, scared, or just needed some comfort. Danni never minded if he came and slept in bed with her. It was innocent enough and after their father died it seemed like his family turned inward to get through the tough times.

The house was designed in a way that put the main bathroom directly across the hall from David's bedroom door. He could hear the shower running and was just imagining what his sister was doing in it. He had a picture

in his mind of warm water and soap running down over her body. He looked up and saw the reflection in the window and noticed the bathroom door was slightly ajar. He could see his sister in the shower from the mirror. The steam and the distance made it look like one big blob, but he could still see a crude female shape. He shifted his gaze back to his homework when he heard her shut off the water. He stole occasional glances of what was going on in the bathroom through the reversed reflection presented in the window glass.

Tina had a towel wrapped around her torso and was drying her hair with another towel. She wiped the steam from the mirror and stood there looking at her reflection. He quickly looked back down at his homework when he noticed that his sister was looking back at him in the mirror. He took one last glance through his peripheral vision as she bumped the door closed with her hip. With the distraction over David returned his focus back to his homework and noticed that he was no further along than he was a half hour ago when his sister had got into the shower. David quickly finished what was left of his chemistry homework and closed his books. At least he had gotten his homework done and he would be able to relax for the rest of the weekend. David stood up and closed his bedroom door and changed into a pair of sweatpants

and a white tank top.

David returned to his desk and turned on his computer. Sitting back down in his chair he loaded up one of his games and started playing. He was so fully engrossed into his game that he hadn't heard Tina enter his room. She walked up slowly behind him and bent down and kissed him on the neck. She had done it so unobtrusively that she caught him by surprise. David quickly lost his focus on the game and his character died.

"I'm sorry" Tina said with a tone of regret. "I didn't mean for that to happen." She put her arms around him again and hugged him. David wasn't sure if she meant the game or the episode at dinner either way he didn't care. He really enjoyed seeing his sister that way, and he wished he had let her remove her bra. But that time had passed and he was certain it wouldn't come around again.

"It's alright I will just re-spawn again." David said then he proceeded to shut down the game and turn off the computer. "You want to watch a movie? I think Ironman is on, or we can watch something else." David said as he tried to ignore the fact that he could feel his sisters nipples harden and push against his back. He definitely didn't mind that feeling one bit, and he wasn't about to move away from her either.

"That sounds fine or we can watch something else if

you want." Tina said not letting go of her brother. She liked the feel of her breasts against his back. She squeezed him a little tighter and then released her grip so that he could stand up. David turned around to see that his sister was wearing a white loose fitting tank top that she often wore to bed sleep in. She had on her favorite pair of flannel pajama bottoms. As she walked out of his room he could easily tell in an instant that she was not wearing panties or a bra. David tried to adjust his semi erect penis so it wasn't noticeable and followed his sister out and into the living room.

David sat down on the couch and grabbed the remote. While Tina flittered around the house turning out the lights and making sure the doors were all locked. Finally after a couple minutes the only light on was coming from the television. Tina grabbed a velour blanket and wrapped it around her shoulders a walked over to the couch and sat down next to her brother. She leaned in next to him and placed her head on his shoulder and covered them both up with the blanket.

"First one to fall asleep first loses." Tina said with a little smile. Loses what? David thought for a moment as he flipped through the channels looking for a movie on cable. He found Ironman on and stopped changing channels. Tina snuggled up a little tighter to David and

settled in to watch the movie.

It was starting to get dark outside and the house was now almost completely black except for the glow coming from the TV. Tina enjoyed these moments alone with her brother more than anything in her life. Ever since the tragedy that destroyed the life they once knew, David had become the one she had leaned on the most. David didn't see it though he always thought it was him leaning on her. It wasn't lost on Tina that her brother David was turning in to one fine looking man. For being sixteen he was without a doubt one of the best looking young men in his class. David ran track and had already broke a few records. He was also on the swim team as well. He was in good shape and had a well-defined body. He didn't have six pack abs, but he still looked good with his shirt off. His blue eyes were like endless pools that women love to get lost in.

David relaxed a little more and leaned into Tina while they sat on the couch. David had seen this movie probably twenty times but he didn't really care. These moments were the only times when he could really just relax and not think about anything. These moments were too few and far between. David put his arm around his sisters shoulders a stretched his legs out a little. They sat there watching the movie in silence. David heard a key in

the door and knew that Danni was home from work. She closed the door and just waved to David and headed to her room. She always worked the opening shift on Saturdays and had to get up early. David looked over to see that Tina was sound asleep on his shoulder. He was getting to hot under the blanket and threw it off his chest in hopes of cooling down a little.

David looked over and noticed that Tina's tank top had moved and was exposing almost all of her breast the only part still covered was her areola. He lowered his arm a bit and realized that he could touch the side of her breast. He could feel the softness of her skin and then continued to slide his hand under her tank top till he had his hand covering her entire breast. He fought back the urge to squeeze her breast and just let his hand rest there. Tina stirred a bit and he quickly pulled his hand out of her top. She turned a little bit and then her head was resting on his chest. Now David could see most of both breasts and he reached out and slipped his hand into her top again. He sat there scared that she might wake up but he also couldn't believe he was touching her breasts.

David laid there forgetting about the movie and focused on his new preoccupation. David had touched breasts before, but it was never quite like this. A few of the girls at school really liked him and he hung out with

then when he had time. Sandy was the first one to let him touch her breasts but she was shy and really small. He remembered that they were barely even there. Mandy was a little bigger and she even let him suck on them for a moment. And then there was Amy and Brie they were twins and they were really cute. They both just took their tops off in front of David and let him fondle them for twenty minutes or so. Then their parents came home and cut their fun before it went any further. None of them came close to the same feeling he was having at this moment.

Keys rattled in the lock again and David quickly removed his hand and covered his sister up with the blanket. David's mother Alyson was just getting home from work. He looked at the clock and noticed it was almost eleven. She locked the door and walked over and gave him a kiss on the cheek.

"Good night dear. Try not to stay up too late; we have to run some errands tomorrow." She said then turned and disappeared down the hall. David sat there shaking slightly from the stress of almost getting caught. When he heard his mother close her bedroom door he knew he was not going to be disturbed any further. He threw the blanket off of him and his sister again. This time in the glow that the TV was casting about the room David could see her

areola and the nipple of her right breast. He rubbed his finger around the nipple in a clockwise motion and it became erect. His sister stirred again but didn't wake up. David was getting braver by the minute he wanted to see and touch more.

David reached down with his other hand and slowly started to pull her tank top up. He pulled it up and was looking at her stomach. He was slowly working her shirt up further and further trying to be careful not to wake her up, but still very determined to get both her breasts free from the cotton prison that was her tank top. After what seemed like forever David finally managed to get her tank top up high enough that her breasts were free. He started to slowly circle the nipples with his finger making them harden and puff up. He then started to gently squeeze them and pinch them between his finger and thumb. His sister made a soft noise of pleasure but still remained sleeping. This just solidified David's confidence even more. David leaned forward a little bit careful not to move Tina too much and reached for the waist of her flannel pajama pants. He reached as far as he could and was able to get his fingertips just inside the waist band.

He stretched further but just couldn't reach the prize he was hoping for. He attempted it a couple more times but just didn't have the length to advance his hand any

further. David resigned to be happy with what he was able to accomplish this evening. He figured that the chance of another opportunity like this happening again was next to zero. He managed to slip his sisters tank top back down and back over her breasts then gently woke her up. Tina slowly opened her eyes and blinked a couple times. She looked at David and then sat up on the couch.

"I guess I lose huh D?" She asked in a low tone. Rubbing her eyes and stretching her legs out. "What do you want for your reward?" She added.

"Let's just call it good. I have been rewarded enough tonight." David said with a little grin. His sister smiled thinking he was talking about the dinner time bra incident and stood up.

"Ok, if you say so." Then she walked down the hall with David. Stopping in front of his bed room door she turned and went to give him a kiss on the cheek. David turned to say goodnight and ended up catching Tina's kiss right on the lips.

"Oh… Ugh… well good night sis." David said a little shocked by the kiss. And then went into his room and shut the door.

Tina continued on to her bedroom and climbed in bed. David lay on his bed but couldn't sleep. He had a massive erection that wouldn't go away and he was still too excited

by the evening's events to fall asleep. He rolled over and grabbed a towel and pulled his cock out of his pants and started masturbating. Within a few minutes he reached orgasm and then cleaned up the evidence with the towel. David was still fixated on the events of the night as they replayed through his head. After about twenty to thirty minutes he finally drifted off to sleep.

CHAPTER 2

Morning came way to quickly for David's liking he was looking up at the ceiling as the daylight was just breaking through the window of his room. He sat up in his bed and rubbed the sleep from his eyes. He turned and placed his feet on the floor as he looked at the clock. It was 5:45 am in the morning, he was sure that nobody else would be up this early and decided a run was a good way to start off his Saturday.

David changed into his running shorts and shoes and put on his long sleeved Under Amour shirt. It was a Hunter Green color and would provide some warmth till he got warmed up. David closed the front door of the house and tied his house key into the laces of his running shoe.

After stretching for a couple minutes he started off up the street at a fast walk. After about ten minutes he

increased his pace to a jog then finally to a run. David was in his own world listening to music on his MP3 player and enjoying the morning. He turned up Hilltop road that started the first mile of what would be a seven mile run.

Hilltop road was a winding climbing and falling road that was challenging for bicyclists let alone runners and it was a favorite route for the cross country running team. The speed limit was posted at 25 MPH and most drivers obeyed it. Mostly because those that didn't either hit deer on the road or ended up leaving the pavement all together.

David knew there wouldn't be anybody out here this early driving on the road. As he settled into his long distance running pace he started to think about the events of the previous night. He was kicking himself for not seeing if his sister was really going to remove her bra at the table. But one thing was for sure he did enjoy touching them and he most definitely wanted to suck on them. He tried to shake the images out of his mind but it was no use.

David was just rounding a blind corner when he collided right into another runner heading the opposite direction. They hit each other with a terrible thud that took them both to the ground. They rolled a few feet down the embankment by the road and came to a stop. They were still tangled together as David slowly started to move his arms and legs to check for injuries. The runner he had

collided into was slowly moving and doing the same thing.

"Would you mind removing your hand from my ass!" she said with a snort. David turned his head to see Molly laying on the ground next to him. David pulled his hand away and moved himself into a sitting position.

"Sorry Molly didn't think anyone else would be up here this early in the morning." David said with a little smirk on his face. Molly turned around to see David sitting there with a scrape on his chin.

"Oh, I'm sorry David I didn't know it was you." She said then gave him a little mischievous grin and added "You can touch my ass anytime." That caught David by surprise and he must have turned a little red cause she just laughed. David stood up and offered his hand to Molly to help her up as well.

"What you doing out so early anyhow?" David asked brushing the dirt and grass off himself.

"I like to run in the mornings when it is cooler." Molly said as she looked David over. He was only a couple inches taller than her and had well defined arms and legs from running and swimming. She definitely liked what she saw, that was for sure. But his melancholy attitude made it hard for her to get close to him. She touched his chin and asked "Does that hurt?"

"No not to bad probably looks worse than it is." David

commented. "Want to run together? I could use the company." He added. You could have knocked Molly over with a feather. She had been trying to get close to David for over a year. Ever since he moved here, and she had seen him for the first time in school. She just couldn't seem to break through his shell.

"Sure. Want me to set the pace, or do you want to?" Molly replied still a little surprised. As she pulled a few weeds out of her hair.

"You go ahead. I'll follow you so we don't have any more accidents." David said.

"Well try to keep up!" Molly replied as she set out running down the side of the road. David followed close behind her keeping perfect pace with her. David liked Molly, she was one of the first people to be nice to him when he moved here and she was definitely easy on the eyes. Like him she was on the track team. She was also on the dive team, and did gymnastics as well. He saw her a few times at the pool since the dive team and the swim team were usually using the facility at the same time. Both pools were in the same building so it was easy to see her there. He always tried not to stare at her so he wouldn't look like a creep. But she really did fill out a bathing suit quite nicely.

Molly stood 5'9" tall to David's 5'11" frame. She had

long blond hair that she always wore in a ponytail or a bun. Depending what she was doing. And her long slender legs were as beautiful as she was. She tended to wear vary little makeup, and as far as David thought she didn't need it anyway. David continued to follow Molly up and down over the hills and corners. He really enjoyed the view from where he was. Strangely enough Molly wasn't really wearing running shorts. The shorts she was wearing were tighter and really showed off her nice tight round little ass. David was almost entranced by it. After about a mile and a half Molly stopped.

"Hang on a second I got to take this off. I think I got something in it." Molly stated as she pulled her jogging bra straps off her shoulders, reaching under her tank top she then proceeded to pull it down over her torso. Finally stepping out of it. David stood there half in shock and half in awe that she would do something like that in front of him. She then smiled at him and threw the sports bra in his face. 'Here you can have it. Bet you can't beat me to Mill Creek." She said as she took off running at top speed down the road.

David stood there for a second just holding the bra in his hand and then took off down the road following after Molly. Mill Creek was just up the road about two miles. There was a small trail that he could take that would cut

about a quarter mile off the distance and put him there before her. David wasn't sure if Molly knew about the shortcut, but it was going to be his ace in the hole.

After about a half mile David had recovered most of the ground he had lost when Molly took off ahead of him. He was barely winded at this point and wasn't pushing himself much at all Molly looked like she wasn't going to be able to keep up her pace. He would easily pass her before too long.

"What do you get if you win?" He yelled to her. Once he got close enough to her.

"You have to buy me dinner." She replied without looking back to see how close David had gotten to her.

"What if I Win? What do I get?" David inquired slowing a little so he wouldn't pass her.

"I'm sure you can think of something." Molly said this time looking over her shoulder.

"Oh I'm sure I can." David added with a hint of sarcasm in his voice. Just then he watched Molly give a burst of speed and turn off the side of the road and head down the trail. Damn, she knows about the trail. I'm going to have to catch her with pure speed now. David thought as he followed her down the trail. David picked up his speed as he tried to close the gap between him and Molly. He knew the trail was just too narrow to try to pass

her. He knew he only had one chance to pass her, and that would be the small clearing up ahead. David could see the clearing coming up ahead and turned on a little extra speed. His muscles were starting to ache now but he was determined to pass Molly.

Molly knew that the clearing was where David would have to pass her. But she also knew she couldn't keep this pace up much longer either. Her legs and arms were burning. She knew she had nothing left in the tank, and David was closing quick her only hope was to clear the distance of the clearing before David could catch her.

David dug deep as he and Molly burst into the clearing. He was right on her heals and was going to get past her. When his foot caught a tree root on the ground and he started to fall. He reached out for anything to help stop his fall, and all that was there was Molly.

Whether on purpose or accident all Molly could feel was a pair of hands hit her and then grab ahold of anything they could find. Then she started to fall as well.

David's natural reaction was no different than anyone else when falling, and that was the hope that he could break his fall. Instinctively he grabbed for anything he could get ahold of. In this case it happened to be Molly's shorts. As the pair continued to fall David was pulling Molly's shorts down with him. They both hit the ground

with a hard thud and came to an abrupt stop. Molly let out a surprised scream when she realized she was no longer wearing her shorts, and David quickly jumped to his feet. He stood there holding Molly's shorts in one hand and her sports bra in the other.

Molly got back to her feet and was standing there facing David. She didn't know what to say, and David didn't know what he should do next. Molly's face had a look of embarrassment as she stood there in front of David. David's eyes got wide as he saw her standing there in her t-shirt and black bikini panties. He wanted to look away but couldn't bring himself to do it. Molly stood there just looking at David. David took a step towards her and the two were face to face. He looked down at Molly and could see her nipples were poking up and straining against her shirt. He opened his hands and let her bra and shorts fall to the ground.

Molly leaned in and pressed her lips to his. To say David was surprised would have been a understatement. He was totally shocked as she pushed her tongue in his mouth. This was a totally new experience for David he had kissed many girls before but he could not recall a single one that had kissed him like this. He grabbed her arms and leaned into her as he attempted to push his tongue into Molly's mouth as well. Molly wrapped her

31

arms around David and pulled her body into his. They were getting lost in the moment and David was enjoying every minute of it. David's thumb moved slightly and found one of Molly's hard nipples pushing against her shirt. He started massaging it as he moved his other hand around to her back.

David placed his hand between her shoulder blades holding Molly tight. As they continued to kiss then he slowly lowered his hand down her back. Within seconds his hand was resting under her t-shirt at the small of her back. David pulled her into him and Molly could feel something poking her leg. David lowered his hand a little more and found the top of her panties. He continued to slide his hand down till it was resting on her bottom. Her skin was so smooth that it was like touching silk. He slowly slid his hand around her side till it was resting on her hip and then lowered his other hand so it was resting on the other hip. Molly knew where David's thoughts were heading; her thoughts were heading in that direction too.

David's fingers slipped inside Molly's panties and he was getting ready to pull them off. When Molly placed her hands on his chest and pushed David away. David lost his balance and ended up falling back and landing on his butt. He sat there looking up at Molly not sure what had just happened. Molly bent down and grabbed her shorts and

pulled them on.

"Sorry, if I didn't stop we might have gone further and I don't want anyone to happen upon us while we were getting to know each other." She said as she straightened out her clothes.

"You're probably right this is a well-used trail." David said nodding his head in agreement. David stood up and was adjusting his shorts, and caught Molly looking at the large bulge in the front. When she noticed he had caught her looking she quickly looked away. David stifled the urge to smile and walked over to Molly.

"So I guess I won. So I get to choose my reward?" David said with a serious look on his face.

"I think you already got your reward." Molly said winking at David. She turned and started to walk down the trail with David following close behind her. They chatted for the short walk down the trail till it opened up at the road again. Molly turned and gave David another kiss.

"I better get going, I have gymnastics practice in an hour." She said. "And you still owe me dinner." She added as she started jogging down the road.

"I thought I won!" David yelled to her.

"That's what you get for thinking." She said just before she turned the corner and disappeared out of his sight.

David jogged off in the opposite direction to finish his

run and head home. He had just turned into his driveway when one of his favorite songs came on his MP3 player. He hated how it always seemed to work like that. David shut off the player and took his headphones out of his ears as he entered the house.

The clock read 7:52. The activities with Molly had caused him to cut his run short but he certainly didn't mind one bit. The house was quiet confirming his suspicion that everyone was still sleeping. Danni of course had already left for work since David hadn't seen her car in the drive way when he got home. David made himself a bowl of cereal and sat down at the table and started flipping through the newspaper.

There was nothing new in the newspaper it was just the same old bad news delivered in a different way. David pushed it way and continued to eat his cereal. Finishing his cereal and put his bowl in the dishwasher and sat back down at the table. He was relaxing and thinking about Molly. Just then David's mother walked around the corner and froze. David looked up and couldn't believe what he was seeing. His mother was standing there wearing just a pair of pink panties and nothing else. His mother always walked around the house dressed. He could count on one hand the number of times he had seen her in her bathrobe.

David just sat there dumbfounded looking at his

mother. She was considerably good looking for a woman of her age. She had long slender legs and a classic hour glass shape. She had shoulder length dark brown hair and emerald green eyes. She was wearing a pair of pink string bikini panties with a pink bow in the middle right below her belly button. Her breasts were full, and round with large brown areola's and large nipples.

His mother turned like she was going to leave then figuring there was nothing that could be undone she turned back around and continued into the kitchen.

"I didn't realize you were already up honey." She said as she walked past him into the kitchen. He continued to follow her turning his head but still remained seated. He noticed that his mother's butt was firm and round. It reminded him of Molly's and he wondered what it must look like in a pair of thong panties. Then he wondered if his mother's skin was a smooth as Molly's was.

She turned and bent over slightly to get a bottle of orange juice out of the fridge. She poured herself a glass and then placed the bottle back in the refrigerator. Grabbing her glass she turned and headed towards her room. Before she turned the corner she looked back at David.

"You going to be ready to go in about an hour?" She asked him.

"Sure, I just need to take a shower and I'll be ready." He said still unable to take his eyes off his mother. David continued to watch her till she disappeared around the corner. The last few days had certainly been strange. First his sister then Molly and now his mother. Trying to wrap his mind around it was giving him a headache. Maybe he had been transported to an alternate reality, or maybe this was all just one big elaborate dream. He pondered the possibilities for a few minutes then just dismissed them with a chuckle. He bumped his chin with his hand and felt the pain from the scratch and what was now going to be a bruise. Well that confirms it is definitely not a dream. He thought as he got up from the table and headed towards the bathroom.

The hot water was welcome relief as it washed over his sore muscles. Obviously running into Molly had caused a little more damage than he had figured. Over all it had been one of the highlights of his week. He wasn't however looking forward to the next eight hours with his mother. After his father had passed and she had to return to work. She had always felt guilty that she wasn't home for the kids like she wanted to be. So she started having these special outings for the kids on the weekends. This happened to be David's weekend. He wasn't sure what she had planned or whether or not he would even enjoy it. But he did

understand the general purpose of it was more for his mother's sake than his, and he was willing to endure almost anything to make her happy.

Their last weekend was antiquing, a museum and lunch. This one could have been anything from the zoo to the science center on maybe even a movie. Trying to figure out what his mother was thinking was an effort in futility. David closed his eyes plunging his head under the shower head and held it there while the visions of Molly ran through his head. He played it out ending several different ways in his mind, and was only succeeding in making himself aroused. After a couple more versions unfolded in his mind; David had to take matters into his own hands and release his pent up frustrations.

David shut off the water and grabbed his towel. He stepped out of the shower while he wrapped it around his waist. He crossed the hall to his bedroom and shut the door.

Alyson stood there looking at her reflection in the full length mirror that was in the corner of her room. She sure didn't think she looked like a middle aged mother of three. And she definitely didn't think she looked forty years old either. There was the slight pooch that was the result of having three kids, but not a single stretch mark. That was a

feat for any pregnant woman and she had been lucky to avoid having any after three children. Her breasts were still firm and round but were starting to sag just slightly. Even if she was the only one that could notice it. Her legs were long and accented her figure nicely they were toned but not overly muscular. A testament to the fact that she worked out at the gym three days a week.

Unfortunately though her dark brown hair was that which was betraying her. It was thinning and strands of grey were starting to poke up here and there. She liked to keep her hair about shoulder length and could wear it several different ways. With her job at the insurance company she found that her hair style changed depending on her duties for the day or week.

She picked up a pink bra that matched her panties and put it on. She adjusted the straps and turned and looked at herself in the mirror again. It was times like these that she really missed her husband. It was rare that he would be able to keep his hands off of her. When she was dressing or undressing he would often walk up behind her and help her with her clothes, whether she needed it or not. She turned her gaze from the mirror and pulled on her pants and then grabbed the white linen shirt she was planning to wear. As she buttoned up the shirt she stopped one button below the collar.

It was uncommon for her to wear a button up shirt without buttoning all the buttons except for the collar. She had to admit that it did feel a bit liberating. But liberating from what was a lot harder for her to pin down. She slipped her feet into a pair of boots and then turned to the mirror to check her appearance one last time. Thomas would have just loved this look on her, he probably wouldn't have been able to keep his hands off of her. She pulled her hair up in a ponytail and turned and walked out of her bedroom.

She grabbed a lightweight coat and set it by the door. Then Alyson walked over to the kitchen and made some toast with peanut butter for breakfast. She seldom ate breakfast during the week because she usually ran out of time with trying to get ready for work and make sure the kids all got off to school on time. Some days she wondered how she was even capable of doing it all. However after Thomas's death she had to step up and do everything. Danni had been 16 when he died and she was able to help her mother quite a bit. She still needed to be a teenage girl though too, and it was hard to watch her give up so much to help her. Tina and David were the ones that seemed to take it the hardest. The sleepless nights she racked up helping David through his nightmares were the worst part of it all. Like any mother she wouldn't have

traded one moment of it, but a part of her seemed to die because she couldn't just make it stop.

Tina weathered it a lot better than David but she still had her scars too. Gone was the outwardly open girl that she had been, and now all that was left was a girl who was closed off to everyone. Her family had certainly been through more heartache than they deserved. She wanted to get them all, herself included professional help but she just couldn't afford it.

Thomas was a great man and a wonderful provider. But at the time of his accident and unfortunate death he left the family with no safety net. Even though he was a Vice President at the First National Bank. He had to make some sacrifices to keep everything running smoothly. One of those sacrifices was the cancelation of their life insurance policies. They had decided when they had children that Alyson would stay home with the kids. Thomas preferred her being home as opposed to the kids being raised by daycare's and baby sitters, and she enjoyed it too.

Their house was a large five bedroom colonial style house in a nice neighborhood. It had been their dream house and she hated to have to sell it and move to this smaller house in Sanderson. She hated that she had to move the family seventy five miles away from their friends

as well. The schools here were very good and she was able to find a good job with the insurance company. She was able to keep food in the house and the bills paid. The tradeoff was that she had to work at least ten hours of overtime every week just to provide some breathing room financially.

She made sure that the kids didn't want for anything but it was hard to keep it from draining her. That is why she enjoyed her weekends. It was a time to spend one on one time with each of the kids. One Saturday each month she and one of the children would go out and do something together. On the fourth weekend of the month she had to work so it evened everything out.

David came out from his room dressed in blue jeans and a button up shirt. Alyson stood there just looking at him. It seemed like every day he looked more and more like his father. Thomas had short cut light brown hair and piercing blue eyes. He stood six feet tall, and was always clean shaven. Although David was slightly shorter and wore his hair in a different style he still looked just like his father. David grabbed a coat and walked over and gave his mother a big warm hug.

"What's that for?" she inquired slightly surprised by the sudden display of affection.

"You just looked like you needed it Mom." David

replied with a smile she had seen a thousand times before it wasn't just his smile it was Thomas's smile as well. They walked out of the house together and got into the car. David had his license and was always looking for anytime he could get behind the wheel, but he thought better of not asking his mother if he could drive.

They drove out of the city talking about any number of topics. School and his grades were always top of the list but today his mother just bypassed the subject. She asked him about girls and if there was anyone in particular he was interested in. David skirted around the question by just saying there were a few he liked but nothing serious. The rest of the drive was pretty much uneventful they talked about this and that but nothing in particular.

After about an hour of driving they turned onto a dirt road and headed towards a farm house. Coming to a stop in what he assumed was a parking area. His mother turned to him and said.

"Here we are." Turning the car off and removing the key as she looked out the window.

"Horses, really mom?" David said in a disheartened tone.

"Come on the least you can do is try it." She said opening the door. "Besides I have never known you for being one to back away from new experiences." She closed

the door behind her.

"Fine you win." David knew it was a lost cause to protest any further as he got out of the car. Besides there could have been a lot more worse things his mother could have chosen.

CHAPTER 3

The next couple weeks were run of the mill. School was going good and David's grades were starting to improve some. He was also spending more time with Molly even though it was hard to find any free time in their schedules. It was Friday and he was ready for the weekend. David was sitting outside the school as usual waiting for his sisters to pick him up. When they pulled up David was lost in his own little world.

"Come on D, we want to get on the road as soon as we can." Tina called to him. Jumping down from the wall he was sitting on David meandered over to the car. Tina got out of the car and pushed David into the back seat and shut the door. Then jumped back into the front seat.

"You would think you two are in a hurry to get rid of me." David said poking fun at his two sisters.

"We've had this planned for almost a month and this is

the first weekend I have had off in two months." Danni said as she took off a little faster than she had planned causing the rear tires of the car to throw dirt and pebbles into the air behind it.

"Easy Mario, We don't need a ticket." Tina added smirking at Danni. "Besides Jarred will still be there when we get there Danni."

"That's not why we are going, and he is just a friend." Danni quipped as her face turned red. "I haven't been skiing in over a year."

"How long a drive is it to Mt. Rose anyway?" David asked hoping to change the topic.

"A little less than 4 hours. So we want to get going as soon as you get out of the car, and we get our gear." Danni replied. They pulled into the driveway ten minutes later and David climbed out and slung his backpack over his shoulder Walking towards the house his sisters followed behind him chattering back and forth among themselves. David took his backpack to his room and dropped it on his bed. He listened as his sisters gathered up their things and loaded them into the car. It was just going to be him and his mother for the weekend, and he was starting to dread what that could possibly entail. David walked into the kitchen to grab a drink from the fridge and saw the sack of food his mom left for his sisters.

He grabbed the bag and took it over to Tina as she was walking out the door.

"Mom left this for you two. Have a good trip." David said handing her the bag.

"Thanks, have a good weekend yourself D." She replied. Then walked out to the car. Danni walked up to David and gave him a kiss on the cheek and headed out the door. Tina came back into the house and grabbed her ski coat. Before she walked out the door she stopped and gave David a big hug. David turned his cheek to her as she went to give him a kiss. Tina moved her head so that her lips touched his, she kissed him and stuck her tongue in his mouth. David was shocked to say the least as Tina just winked at him and turned to walk out the door.

"That's how you kiss a woman goodbye." She said to him over her shoulder. David just watched her get into the car and wave as they drove off. Well that's not what I would have expected. David thought to himself.

David walked into the kitchen and got himself a glass of milk out of the refrigerator, and headed to his room to do his homework. He finished his homework a little after five o'clock and noticed that it was starting to get dark. David headed to the kitchen and set the oven to 400 degrees. He looked at the phone and wanted to call Molly and invite her over since he had the house all to himself

for the next several hours. However she was out of town visiting her grandparents who were celebrating their 60th anniversary.

David pulled a frozen pizza out of the freezer and unwrapped it. Placing it on a pizza pan he slid it into the oven and set the timer for fifteen minutes. He returned to the refrigerator and grabbed the items to make a salad and put them on the counter. He made himself a salad and placed the unused ingredients back into the fridge and closed the door. He poured Italian dressing over his salad and set it on the table as the timer went off. He pulled the pizza out of the oven and set it on the cutting board and grabbed the pizza cutter. Well this is one pathetic dinner he thought to himself as he ran the cutter across the pizza. Definitely not one of his healthier options. But he tried to give himself a couple of luxury items a week just to keep the insane cravings away. Buffalo wings would go great with this he thought as he finished cutting up the pizza.

David sat at the table eating his pizza and salad. He thought about taking it and eating on the couch in the living room, but that was forbidden by his mother. Besides with his luck he would drop something and make a stain that he couldn't hide. As David continued to eat his dinner he found himself thinking about Molly. She was definitely taking up more and more of his cerebral

processes lately.

They had a couple classes together at school and he enjoyed getting to see her. Their after school activities however kept them apart for the most part. They would still meet on Saturdays to run together and David enjoyed that time they had alone together. Last weekend after their run she invited him back to her house.

When they got there she acted surprised like she didn't know her parents weren't going to be home. David thought it was an act and just went along with it as they entered her house. She offered him a drink and then gave him a tour of the house. Conveniently the tour ended in her bedroom. It was a typical teen girls room the walls were painted off-white and she had a full size bed piled with pillows and stuffed animals on top. Along one wall ran a shelf with trophies and medals that she had won in gymnastics competitions.

Molly sat down on the side of her bed, while David took a seat in the chair in front of her computer desk. David studied her face as she took a drink from her water glass. She had this mischievous look in her eye. David's mind raced imagining all the things that could possibly be going through that pretty little head of hers. Trying to second guess a woman was an impossible task. Upon

being forced into the role of man of the house and living with not only his mother but his two sisters. It was a lesson he had learned hard, fast and often.

"What are you thinking about?" Molly broke the silence first.

"Just how pretty you look." David said with a coy smile on his face.

"Yea right, I'm sweaty, smelly, and have no makeup on. There is no way I look pretty." She retorted back at him.

"Then get cleaned up." David motioned to the bathroom with his head. "I don't really care though, I'm sweaty and smelly too." smiling back at her.

"OK" she set her glass down on the nightstand and stood up pulling her t-shirt off over her head. "You want to join me?" she added as she tossed it over to the clothes basket by her closet door. Before David could say anything she pulled her sports bra up over her head and tossed it on top of her t-shirt.

David sat there just looking at her. He wasn't sure what he should do next. He stood up from the chair and stepped towards her.

"I have another idea" David said as he closed the distance between them. Molly stood her ground not moving an inch. As David stepped up to her and placed his hands on her waist. David kissed her on the lips and

pushed his tongue into her mouth. She willingly opened her mouth and returned in kind. David moved his hand up and was soon cupping her firm breast in it. Her breast felt soft and warm, still slightly moist from sweat. He ran his thumb over the top of the nipple and it instantly puffed up and stuck out straight. David continued to kiss and fondle Molly enjoying every minute.

Molly was surprised by David's forwardness this was in stark contrast to the reserved nature he presented in school and she really liked this side of him much better. David was waiting for Molly to push him away but it didn't happen. He continued to kiss her and touch her bare chest. After a few moments David moved and kissed her on the chin and then down her jaw line to her neck. He slowly kissed moving down her neck and across her collar bone to her shoulder.

He pushed Molly back against her bed and followed her body as she fell back onto it. He continued to kiss across her chest as he had recalled seeing in some movie. David assumed he was doing something right as all he heard from Molly was gasps, ooh's and ah's. David eventually reached her breasts and started to gently kiss them. Starting with one and then the other he moved back and forth between them. Her nipples were sticking straight upright and David placed his lips over one and then

sucked gently on it. Molly reached up and grabbed the back of David head pulling him against her chest.

David was shocked at first unsure if he had done something wrong or not. Seeing that Molly wasn't pushing him away confirmed his suspicions that she was enjoying it as much if not more than he was. David continued to kiss and suck on her breasts taking his time trying to think about what he was doing and what he should try next.

Molly laid there enjoying every moment she was having with David. He was the first boy she had kissed let alone let see her topless. But here in her room on her bed the two of them were experiencing something they both wanted. Molly could feel something pressing against her leg and could tell that David was enjoying it as much as she was.

David slowly started to kiss down Molly's stomach and stopped at the waist band of her shorts. He proceeded to travel back up her body kissing as he went till he found her mouth once again. David wasn't sure how far Molly was going to let him go but he knew he had to see just how far he could get. As they laid on the bed kissing David moved his hands down to Molly's hips. He grabbed her shorts and pulled them down slightly. He was surprised that she didn't try to stop him. With another tug or two her shorts were laying on the floor next to the bed.

Molly laid there on the bed wearing nothing else but a green lacey pair of thong panties. David stopped and was just admiring the view. Her fit body was beautiful to just behold, and he was slowly looking over her burning the very image in to his brain. This was a sight he wasn't sure he would get the chance to see soon; or ever again. It was one that he definitely wanted to remember.

David reached for her panties he could see the goal in sight and Molly was showing no signs of stopping him. He had just grasped them at her hips when they heard a strange whirring sound coming from another part of the house.

"Oh crap my parents are home!" came from Molly's lips as she bolted upright. David surprised saw nothing but a bright light and pain as their heads slammed into each other. David rolled off the bed and on to the floor. As his vision cleared he watched Molly pull her shorts on and then her t-shirt.

"Don't just lay there get up! If my dad catches you in my room I'll be grounded till I'm 30." Molly said with a look of terror on her face. She pushed David's water glass into his hand, and grabbed his arm and pulled him behind her out the door. They no sooner had sat down on the couch when the door opened and in walked her parents.

"Hi Mom and Dad. We just finished our run and were

getting a drink of water." Molly volunteered before they had even got through the door. Her mother just looked at her then over to David. David had the deer in the headlights look on his face as he tried to regain his composure.

"Molly, you know you are not supposed to have company over if we are not home." Her mother stated as she gave David a cautionary glance.

"Mom, this is David. He is on the track team with me. He is also on the Swim team and Cross Country team as well." Molly quickly added not letting her mother continue on her train of thought. "We just finished our seven mile trail run and were both very thirsty so I had him come in to get a drink." She continued. "We have only been here a couple minutes." She paused long enough to take a breath then continued. "David, this is my Mom, Heather and my Dad, Rick."

"Pleased to meet you both." David said as he stood up to shake their hands. "Sorry I didn't mean to get Molly in trouble we were both just parched. It won't happen again." Turning back to look at Molly he could see that her erect nipples were easily visible through her t-shirt.

"Well that's ok now that we have met you. You are welcome to come by anytime." Heather said as she shook his hand.

"I am sorry I can't stay though I have a full schedule today. It was really nice to meet you." David said as he turned for the front door. "I will see you at school Molly" he added as he opened the door. "Have a good day." Closing the door behind him David made his way quickly to the end of the driveway, down the street, and around the corner.

David swallowed his last bite of pizza, and took the dishes into the kitchen. After rinsing them and placing them in the dishwasher he put the soap in and started it. I wonder what I should do now. He thought to himself. Finally he decided that a shower would feel good and then he would see what was good on Cinemax.

David got out of the shower and changed into a pair of sweats and a tank top. He walked out and sat down on the couch and turned on the TV. As he flipped through the channels he wondered what his sisters were doing right then. He wondered if they had made it to Mt. Rose safely. He tended to think about those things a lot since his father had died. He figured he would have heard something by now if there had been anything that had happened. He still kicked himself for not telling Tina to call when she got there just to let him know they made it safely. He tried to push the thoughts out of his mind and focus on the TV.

He found Night Shift Nurses on Cinemax and figured that would be good enough entertainment for the evening. He always found it funny how Cinemax became a soft porn movie station about nine o'clock at night on the weekends. He settled in and started watching the movie. It was a typical porn light on story and long on sex. But it was effective at getting him aroused. Which was the whole purpose of pornography anyway. Once the movie was over David flipped over to the Travel Channel and watched Ghost Adventures. David looked at the clock and saw it was after eleven o'clock and wondered why his mother hadn't gotten home yet. He stretched his legs out on the couch and continued watching TV.

David was awoken at about two fifteen in the morning by a loud bang and laughing. He rolled off the couch and stretched, he could hear his mother laughing as she came up the walk way to the house. He could hear her fumbling with her keys as a car drove off down the road. He walked over to the door as his mother finally managed to get it unlocked and practically fell into the house. David caught her and kept her from hitting the floor. She was still laughing and David could tell she was extremely drunk.

"Thank you, my big strong man." Alyson said as she tried to stand up.

"Mom, are you drunk?" David asked knowing full well

that she was. She just looked at him and smiled then laughed some more. She smelled of alcohol and she was slurring her words heavily. David left her leaning against the wall as he went into the living room and turned the TV off. He walked back over to his mother who had slid down the wall and was now sitting on the floor.

"Come on Mom let's get you to bed." David said as he tried helping her up from the floor.

"That's the best idea I've heard all night Thomas." She said as she slowly stood up then collapsed into his arms. David just let it go that she called him by his father's name. He helped her walk down the hall and into her bed room. Just as they entered the room she stumbled again and the two of them fell onto the bed. David laid there for a second and then got up from the bed.

"Good night mom I'll see you in the morning." David said as he turned for the door.

"Can you help me get undressed." The words slurred out of her mouth. David let out a sigh then turned back facing his mother. "It's not like you to not want to get me out of my clothes anyhow Thomas." she added as she laid on the bed

"Fine, I guess I can help you." David muttered under his breath as he stepped over to the bed. Helping his mother get to an upright sitting position on the side of the

bed he grabbed her shoes and tossed them through the walk-in closet door. She stood up as David reached around her waist and found the button at the back of her skirt. He unfastened the button, and then pulled the zipper down. This was definitely a unusual experience for David. He never thought in a million years that he would have to be helping his mother get undressed.

He pulled at the hips of her skirt and it fell down to the floor. He was surprised to find his mother wearing thigh high stockings and a garter belt. He paused for a moment stunned. He had seen these before in the movies on Cinemax but never in real life.

"Unfasten the clips at the top first." She instructed. "Then roll the stockings down Thomas." David did as he was told disregarding her using his father's name yet again. Once David removed her stockings he proceeded to remove her garter belt and set it on the dresser. She sat back down on the side of the bed. David came back over and waited a moment hoping his mother would tell him to leave.

"Aren't you going to help me with my shirt?" the words tumbling from her lips. David reached up and started unbuttoning her blouse. Button by button he proceeded down over her chest and then her stomach. Till her shirt was open and then pushed it off of her shoulders

and then placed it in the clothes hamper in the closet. David was starting to feel uneasy with his mother sitting there in her bra and panties.

"Do you need any more help mom?" he asked wishing he had kept his mouth shut.

"I'm still wearing clothes aren't I? Besides you always preferred I slept nude anyway Thomas." her words heavily slurred. David just let out a sigh and stepped over to his mother. Before he could do anything she stood up and turned her back to him. He figured this was best since he would only have to look at her back and reached up and unfastened her bra. It was a black strapless style that fell away almost instantly. He set it on the bed then reached for her black panties where they sat on her hips. Just as he touched them she reached out and grabbed his hands and pulled them up and placed them on her breasts and held them there.

David felt awkward but didn't try to pull away. With her hands over his she proceeded to make him massage her breasts. His chest was pressed against her back and he just stood there unsure what he should do next. After a few minutes she let go of his hands and David lowered them to her panties and he slowly pulled them down. Once they were off he grabbed her bra and placed them both in the hamper with the rest of her clothes. David

emerged from the closet just in time to see his mother completely naked climb into the bed and slip under the covers. David turned off the lamp in the corner of the room and turned for the door.

"Good night Mom." David said as he started for the door.

"Will you lay down with me Honey?" came the reply from the bed. David paused then stepped over to the side of the bed.

"OK, Until you fall asleep." David protested as he climbed into the bed. The last place he wanted to be lying was in bed with his naked mother. He told himself that she would be asleep soon and he would then head off to his bedroom.

"Can you take off that damn tank top it is making me itch." She complained to him as he laid there. David obliged his mother wishes and took off his tank top and dropped it on the floor next to the bed. David laid there for another couple minutes in silence waiting for his mother to drift off to sleep or pass out whichever came first he didn't really care as long as it was soon.

"Take them damn sweats off they are making me itch too." came another protest from his mother. Reluctantly David obliged his mother's request even though he wasn't even touching her. She will be asleep any moment now

and I can go to my room and forget this all happened. David thought to himself. A few more minutes passed and David was about to try to make his escape when he heard his mother say "I'm cold slide over here and warm me up Thomas."

David didn't try to object to her newest request. Instead he just slid over next to his mother and placed his arm across her waist and pressed his chest against her back.

"mmm." emitted from his mother's lips. They laid there motionless for a few more minutes. David was feeling warm and comfortable as he laid there he wondered if this would be what it felt like if he was in bed with Molly. Soon he succumbed to the assault of sleep. David was barely awake ten minutes later as he felt something tugging on his stiffening penis. Without opening his eyes he reached out and felt his hand pushed downward. To his surprise he felt a little patch of hair and then a slight warm depression. He pressed his fingers in a little and felt a warm wet round button. Sliding his hand down further he found the prize of his quest and slid his finger into the warm wet hole. The hand on his now erect cock just held it for a moment as he proceeded to slide his finger in and out of the hole he had found.

He heard a familiar voice utter a stifled noise of

enjoyment as he continued. Within moments the body he was laying against turned to face him and then slid his hard cock into the now dripping wet area he was just feeling with his fingers. He rolled over on top of the body and felt two hands grab his buttocks and pull it towards itself. In seconds he took over control and was thrusting himself into this body as sounds of pleasure emitted from it.

She pulled her legs up and wrapped them around his waist as David found a rhythm and pace that felt good to him. He kept his eyes closed as he concentrated on the warm flesh surrounding his manhood. After several more minutes he felt the familiar feeling of release as he climaxed.

"Oh my god." His mother exclaimed as she squeezed her legs tight around him. David thrust himself into her a couple more times then stopped. David opened his eyes immediately and found himself staring his mother in the face. She gave him a kiss and wrapped her arms around him. She released her legs from around his waist. She just laid there looking up into David's face not saying a word just smiling.

David was shocked and didn't know what to say. He just looked at his mother as she looked back at him. He felt himself slip out from inside her and then rolled over to the side. Lying next to his mother he just kept telling

himself that this had to be a dream; a very, very bad dream. Without saying a word his mother sat up leaned over him and took his penis in her hand and then in to her mouth. The hot wetness of her lips on it made him get hard all over again. He laid there as she proceeded to lick and suck on his ridged cock. Taking every inch of it into her mouth and swirling her tongue around it. Her mouth traveled the entire length of his cock up and down repeatedly.

David just laid back enjoying the feeling and before he realized it he was climaxing once again. To his surprise his mother just continued to suck on him taking everything he was giving her. Once he was done she just continued to work it like before till he got hard once more. David reached up and slid his hand up the inside of his mother's thigh and found her warm wet mound. She let out a loud mmm as he slid his finger inside her and then he pushed a second finger inside. He felt her wet juices release over his fingers. He proceeded to push his fingers inside her pushing faster and faster as she made noises of enjoyment.

Suddenly his mother stopped sucking and sat up turning around she straddled him and buried his tool deep inside her as she lowered herself down onto it. She started to slide up and down on his hard cock moaning with each thrust. David was mesmerized by the sight of her breasts bouncing up and down with her movements. He reached

up and grabbed ahold of them as she continued her riding of his manhood. After several more minutes she was sliding all the way up to the tip then dropping herself down hard on top of him as she started to moan louder.

David felt a large rush of liquid cascade from his mother as she let out a loud scream as she proceeded to bounce up and down harder and faster on him. Within a matter of another minute or so David was having another large ejaculation of his own.

"That feels wonderful Thomas." His mother said as she collapsed on top of David then rolled over on her side. David thought that his mother must have been sleep walking or something because she kept calling him by his father's name. David laid there next to his mother wondering what he should do next. He wanted to leave but he also was enjoying his first sexual experience. Compared to masturbating this was definitely more enjoyable, and judging by his mother's reaction she was enjoying it just as much as he was.

He rolled on to his side and pressed his chest against her back and draped his arm over her and rested his hand on her breast. Her breast was so big he could barely hold all of it in his hand. Compared to his sister his mother wore a 38 DD bra. Her skin was soft and warm, gliding his thumb across her nipple he felt it react and stiffen. She

moved slightly giving him more access to her naked frame. He laid there next to her just massaging her breast while he looked at her. His mind was a mass of jumbled thoughts and actions.

After a few moments he leaned in and took her nipple into his mouth and started to suck on it. A sigh escaped from his mother's lips as she laid there. David then bit down lightly on her nipple with his teeth and pulled slightly.

"Oh Yes!" his mother yelled. Then bit her lower lip.

David continued to explore her body with his hands and mouth as she laid there reacting to his every touch. Eventually he made his way down her body till he came to the short cut mound of hair just above her vagina. He could smell the sweet aroma and the warmth radiating from it. He paused slightly then drove his mouth down and onto her mound He pushed his tongue between the folds and tasted the juices. His mother uttered something then pushed his head down further between her thighs. David wasn't positive what he was supposed to be doing and was trying to mimic what he had seen done on the Cinemax movies he had seen. Judging by his mother's reactions he must have been doing something right.

After several minutes he heard her let out a long moan that trailed off into a scream and fluid drenched onto his

tongue and mouth. He looked up and could see her chest heaving with heavy breathing. David rubbed her moist folds with his hand as he moved up next to her side again. His mother let out a couple long breaths then rolled over onto her stomach. David started rubbing her back and traveled from her shoulders down to her buttocks. He gave her ass a squeeze and she just giggled. He moved his hands down to her thighs and was surprised when she opened her legs for him.

The moonlight through the bed room window glistened off the sweat on her bare round derriere. David sat there just admiring it for a moment then he slapped it with his hand. She giggled again and shook her behind a little. David was once again erect as he straddled his mother's legs. She felt his member slide across her gluteus and then fall right into the cleft between them as he slid down further. She lifted up her hips slightly as she felt him find her moist spot once again and push it fully inside her. She stifled a squeal of pleasure as she pushed her pelvis back against him.

Reaching down David grabbed his mother's sides and felt the ridge of her hip bones. His fingers curled around them like a natural handle. He pulled her into himself and then up repositioning his legs so he was in the middle and her legs were spread apart. Still holding her hips he started

to pull himself out and then pushed back in. His mother buried her face into a pillow as he started moving faster and harder into her. Her hips were growing sore from his grasp which got tighter and tighter as he moved. He started slamming himself into her harder and harder and she wasn't sure how much more abuse she could take. Just then she felt herself reach the point of full enjoyment and burst. David let out a few grunts and groans as she screamed out in pure ecstasy. She felt David explode inside her for a fourth time and then his grip released her hip bones which were burning by this time.

David slid out from inside her and he collapsed beside her on the bed. Within a few minutes she heard the familiar sound of snoring. She rolled onto her back and laid there for a few moments till either from exhaustion or over consumption of alcohol she passed out.

David opened his eyes to the sun pouring in from the window on the north wall. He blinked a few times trying to clear the sleep from his eyes and fully wake up. He looked up and saw the ceiling. That was one crazy dream I had last night. He thought to himself as he continued to study the ceiling. He rolled over to his right and noticed that he was looking at the dresser in his mother's bedroom. Startled he jumped out of the bed and almost

ran into the door. He turned around quickly and caught his reflection in his mother's full length dressing mirror. He paused for a second. Well this is my mother's room and I am naked. I guess that was no dream. David pieced the bits of the previous night together that he could recall. He looked down and found his clothes on the floor. He picked them up and quietly stepped out of the room. Leaving his mother still asleep in the bed.

David spent an unusually long time in the shower that morning. He was confused as to what he should do. So many things went through his mind. Most of all he couldn't believe he had just had sex with his mother. He ran through all the events in his mind. His mother kept calling him his father's name., and that puzzled him. Maybe she was so plastered that she didn't know what she was doing, or maybe it was some sort of sleepwalking thing like he had seen in the movies.

David put his head under the spray of the showerhead and tried to put everything out of his mind. Finally after several minutes of analyzing the nights events he decided that he would just keep his mouth shut and wouldn't say anything to his mother. With any luck he hoped that she would not remember anything from the previous night.

Alyson opened her eyes, the sun coming through the

window causing considerable pain. Lifting her head she scanned the room. She was relieved to find that she was in her own house. Her head was pounding and her tongue felt like someone had used it to wipe out a dirty ashtray or three. She sat up in bed hoping that would help clear the fog in her head.

The previous night had been a celebration. After a year of hard work and working 60 hour weeks. She finally got the promotion to District Manager. After work she and her collogues had gone out to have a drink. Quickly one turned into two, and then two turned into four. Before she realized it, it was two a.m. in the morning and the bar was closing down.

She was drunker than two skunks and in no condition to drive. A few of her friends who hadn't been drinking came up with a plan one would drive them to her house. And the other would follow in her car. Then they would take him back to get his car. Fifteen minutes later she was standing on her porch trying to enter the house like a plastered teenager trying to avoid waking her parents. That was the last thing she could clearly recall.

Reaching up she ran her fingers through her hair pulling it back out of her face. She looked down as the sheet and blanket fell away and noticed she was nude. She strained her memory trying to recall what had gone on.

She pulled the bedding back and turned to get out of bed. Standing she felt sore and walking made it worse. As she past in front of her mirror she noticed four red marks evenly spaced out on both of her hips. She touched them and they were sore but not too painful. She continued past the mirror and into her bathroom.

She grabbed her bottle of aspirin and the rattling of the pills inside it made her head pound worse. She opened it and quickly took two of them. Then she thought a moment and took two more before she climbed into the shower. The warm water cascading over her body was refreshing, and it was soothing her soreness as well. She plunged her head under the spray and let the water run down over her.

As she washed her body the shower was helping clear the fog from her mind. Slowly the memories and the visions of the previous night came back to her. Suddenly she was recalling David undressing her and then both being in bed together. The visions flashed through her mind like a movie in a theater. First David on top of her, and then her on top of him. She was shocked as each new vision came to her. Then finally the vision of her son taking her from behind. At that point the marks on her hips and the soreness all made sense to her.

Alyson stood in the shower paralyzed by the shock of

the revelation. This was not the type of relationship she wanted with her children. She herself was not a stranger to the family love lifestyle. She was sixteen years old when she was introduced to it by her father. Even though it was conventional, it wasn't the kind of lifestyle that she wanted for her children. While society called it amoral and deviant, the truth was something totally different. Most family love partakers were warm, loving, and protected families. Even though it was still a lifestyle that had to be lived in secret and hidden from the world.

She had a healthy loving relationship with her father, brothers, and cousins for years. When she moved away to college and met Thomas that part of her life ended. It wasn't till about three years into their marriage that she finally opened up to Thomas about that part of her life. While she knew he didn't really understand it he didn't ostracize her over it either. After all these years she thought that part of her past life was over with.

Alyson turned the shower off and grabbed her towel. She continued to ponder how she was going to handle this situation. She finished drying herself off and then wrapped the towel around her body. She looked at her reflection in the mirror. The results of the prior nights drinking was still evident by the dark circles under her eyes and the pounding in her head. She wanted to just climb

back into bed and sleep it off. That however wasn't an option right now.

She hung her towel up on the rack and stepped through the door to her bedroom. Based on how she was feeling she knew she wasn't going to be leaving the house at all today. She grabbed a pair of pink string bikini panties out of the drawer and her favorite pair of sweat pants. Pulling them on she grabbed a loose fitting grey t-shirt out of another drawer and pulled it on. She briefly contemplated putting a bra on, but then decided she didn't need the added constriction around her torso. Opting for comfort she slipped her feet into a pair of slippers and headed towards the kitchen.

CHAPTER 4

David sat at the table staring down into his bowl of Froot Loops not wanting to make eye contact with his mother. Alyson poured herself a bowl of Froot Loops as well and sat down at the table across from David. They sat there in silence eating their breakfast neither one wanting to be the first to speak. David didn't know what to say or if he should even bring up the topic. Alyson knew that they would have to have a talk about the previous night's events, but wasn't sure how to start the conversation.

"Did you have a good time last night?" David finally said breaking the silence.

"Yes, It was nice to get out and let off some steam. Besides I had good news yesterday. I got the District Manager promotion I was trying for." She stated then continued "So I was celebrating with some of my co-workers last night. I think it might have gotten a little out

of hand. Matter of fact I am kind of hangover."

"Congratulations Mom, I know you have been working hard to get that position. Does that mean you won't have to work so many hours?" David inquired happy to be avoiding the obvious topic.

"Well I will have more work to do, but I will have to work some overtime just not like I have been. There will also be times when I will have to be out of town overnight." She revealed.

"That's OK, we are old enough to take care of ourselves now anyhow Mom." David declared "Besides Tina acts like a Mom half the time anyways, and Danni fills in where she leaves off." He followed with a smile.

Alyson cracked a smile then started laughing. David laughed right along with her for a few moments. It was nice to see his mother relaxed for a change. He knew it had to be hard on her being a widow and single mother trying to make sure everything was taken care of. His sisters knew that finances were tight for his mother. That was part of the reason Danni worked as much as she did even though she was in school. Tina wanted to work too but Danni insisted she wait till after she left for college so that David wouldn't be left alone at home that much. So Danni took it upon herself to work at least 30 hours a week often more.

Since their mother would never accept the money from Danni directly. Danni would do things to make it easier for their mother. It had been almost four months before their mother realized that Danni was paying the power company directly for the house power bill. When his mother had finally found out she broke down in tears telling Danni that she didn't have to do that. Danni just said that it was part of being a family, and that they all had to pull together for everyone's sake.

In honesty if Danni hadn't been doing that the power company would have turned the power off. That would have just been one more thing to add to their mothers already overflowing plate. On the plus side though it seemed that for the past three or four months things had progressively gotten better. His mother had gotten a raise and then now a promotion. Things were finally starting to turn towards the better.

David and his mother sat there in silence eating their cereal. David wondered if his mother remembered anything about last night. He almost wanted to ask her about it, but on the other hand he was also content to just forget about it altogether. What if his mother hadn't remembered anything at all about what had transpired. Then his bringing it up would not only be awkward but

also troubling. He finally decided that it was best to keep his mouth shut and forget the whole thing even happened.

David looked down and realized he had reached the bottom of his bowl of cereal and just sat staring at the bit of milk and debris left behind.

"You know there is nothing wrong with what happened." Alyson proposed as she took another bite of her cereal. David looked up his gaze meeting hers with a look on his face that implied he thought he had misheard her.

"It is normal between people that love each other. I love you with all my heart just as I love your sisters." She added taking another bite letting David process her words. The confusion was apparent on his face as he tried to make sense of what he was hearing.

"However this is something that we cannot speak about outside of our family. There are people that are not as accepting of these things." His mother implored as she ate another spoonful of cereal.

"So there is something wrong with what happened then?" David asked with a look of fear upon his face.

"Not at all, it is just that some people regard it as taboo in spite of how normal it is." She answered

David stood up and carried his dishes to the kitchen and placed them in the dish washer.

"So this is normal for this kind of stuff to happen in families?" David inquired trying to wrap his mind around everything.

"Well not in every family, but it isn't uncommon either." She said nonchalantly as she took another bite of cereal.

David was trying to process everything in his mind. It was so confusing and the more he thought about it the more confused it made him. He stood in the kitchen just looking at his mother as she continued to eat her cereal. He finally decided to just let it all go for the time being. His mom was telling him it was OK and she was so relaxed about it that he had no reason to doubt what she said. After a few moments she finished eating and stood up and walked toward the kitchen where David was still standing.

David watched his mother as she walked towards the kitchen. She was wearing her favorite pair of sweat pants and grey t-shirt. It was her stay at home outfit. Her pants were a pale yellow color; faded from being laundered so many times. The repeated washings had also caused them to be thin as well. They were so thin in fact that he could almost see completely threw them.

He could see the pink string bikini panties that his mother was wearing. It wasn't just the outline he could tell

they were pink even when covered by the yellow sweat pants. He could make out the difference in color as the edge was a darker pink than the rest of the material. He followed the line as it crossed up over her buttocks up to her hip and then around her side. David was captivated by what he was looking at. He had seen his mother wear these pants several times before and never noticed how thin they actually were.

The old grey t-shirt was not any better. It like the pants it had been laundered to the point it was almost see through as well. He could easily make out the color difference between her areolas and the rest of her breasts. As if that wasn't enough he could see that her nipples were ridged poking against the shirt. David's mind flashed back to the previous night. He was recalling his mother's body and what it looked like in the darkened room. Now in the morning light he could see even more detail despite the fact that she was wearing clothes.

She stepped past him to the sink and rinsed out her bowl and then placed it into the dishwasher. David just stood there looking at her butt while she bent over placing the bowl in the dishwasher.

"Is it something we might do again?" David asked. He couldn't believe the words even came out of his mouth. Alyson stood up and turned to face him.

"If you want to of course we can. But that is your choice not mine. Going forward it is always going to be your choice honey." She said as she kissed him on the cheek. "So you have any plans for today?"

"No, just thought I would hang out at home today. It don't look like you have any plans either." David replied.

"So I guess it is just us then today huh?" Alyson said shrugging her shoulders. She stepped over to David and gave him a big hug. "I love you very much honey." She said.

David wrapped his arms around his mother hugging her back. Then his hands dropped down to her hips and rested there. His mother relaxed her arms as they just stood there. David stepped to the side and slid his hand up underneath her shirt till he found her breast. He glided his hand over it and then to the nipple which was still sticking out straight. His mother leaned back against the counter and just closed her eyes.

David continued with his exploration using his other hand to push her shirt up over her breasts.

"You can just take it off if you want." She said not opening her eyes just enjoying the moment. David pushed the t-shirt up over her head and let it drop onto the floor. David moved his mouth down to one of her erect nipples and started sucking on it as he rubbed both breasts with

his mother's hips he turned her to face the counter and slid his now fully erect cock deep into his mother from behind. Without objection she bent forward over the counter to give him full access to her body. Grabbing her hips He proceeded to start slamming himself deep inside her. It was just as warm and wet just as he recalled from the night before.

Within moments David found his rhythm and grabbed a hold of her left shoulder. He held on tight as he used it for leverage while he continued pounding away.

"Oh God, OH God, Yes, Harder. Fill me up." Alyson started yelling. David was shocked but didn't stop. He continued to slam his body deep into hers. Moving faster and pushing harder he picked up his rhythm. After a few more minutes he heard his mother let out a scream of pleasure as a hot mass of liquid exploded over him. Without stopping he picked up his pace and moved faster till he reached climax. Alyson could feel him explode inside her as he continued to pound her from behind then he stopped.

Alyson collapsed onto the counter breathing heavily. "No, not yet." She said as David started to pull himself out. David stopped and then pushed himself back against her. David stared down at his mother's bare bottom. It was round and a creamy white color he could make out the

faint tan line across her buttocks. Then all of a sudden a revelation occurred to him.

"What about pregnancy?" David asked his mother as he stepped back abruptly pulling himself out of her.

"It's OK Honey, I can't get pregnant anymore." She said "I had my tubes tied after you were born. So there is no way that could happen." She added as she propped herself up on her elbows. David stood there pondering what his mother had just said. Then he reached out and put his hands around her torso till his hands found her breasts. Cupping each one in his hands he pulled her to him.

She leaned back pressing her back into his chest. She could feel him starting to stiffen against her derriere as he softly massaged her breasts.

"I'm guessing you're not done yet?" She whispered. David just kissed the back of her neck and continued massaging. She felt him grow stiffer as his slick wet member pushed against the cleft of her backside. "I can tell you are enjoying yourself but maybe we should head back to the bedroom. I'm not as young as I use to be and its definitely more comfortable." David didn't utter a word just continued his messaging while he and his mother walked from the kitchen back to her bedroom.

Walking through the door the edge of the bed came up

quicker than they had expected. Both of them were focused on other things as they lost their balance and came down in a combined mass onto the bed. Alyson started laughing with David joining her. She rolled over onto her side so she was now facing him. David just laid there studying her body.

He could make out the tan outline of a bikini top. Which puzzled him since the only time he ever seen his mother in a bathing suit it was always a one piece.

"What are you thinking?" She asked. As she just laid there staring back at him.

"Nothing really. This is just kind of unexpected is all." David said casting his gaze down her body stopping at the moderate tuft of hair above her pubis.

"I know this is a lot to absorb. But it is nothing to worry yourself about." She replied.

David scooted up closer to his mother and ran his hand down her side. Alyson rolled on to her back as David's hand slid across her stomach. Leaning over David looked at the creamy white skin of her firm round breasts as his lips found her nipple. He gently started sucking on it while he slid his hand down to her moist pussy. Willingly his mother opened her legs allowing him complete access.

He felt her hand pushing his head against her breast. A stifled mmmm escaping from her lips as he continued. He

swirled his tongue around her nipple and then bit on it lightly with his teeth.

"Oh My God!" she blurted out in a pained tone.

Surprised David pulled away quickly "Did I hurt you?" he said alarmed.

"No honey its ok. It hurt just a little, but it was a good hurt. Besides I'm a lot tougher that you might think." She said winking at him with a devilish grin on her face. Pushing David back onto his back she climbed on top of him. Using one hand she guided his rock hard member into her as she lowered herself down.

Leaning back she looked him in the eyes. "Let me do some work now." She said as her muscles contracted around his cock. Slowly she lifted herself up and then back down feeling him buried deep inside her. She continued in the same movements slowly gaining speed as David just laid there watching her. She was moving at a methodical pace feeling him fully inserted inside her. She felt herself getting wetter as she continued.

David just laid their watching his mother as she rode him. He was mesmerized just watching her breasts bounce. While she continued her pleasurable activities. David reached up grabbing her hips and pulling her down hard as he thrust his pelvis upward. A scream uttered from her lips as the pleasurable pain shot through her.

David felt himself hit something as he drove himself deep inside her. He stopped instantly with fear.

"Did I hurt you?" He inquired with a look of concern upon his face.

"No, It's ok just been a long time since someone has gone that deep. It will be fine." She said as she kept moving her hips back and forth atop of him.

She continued her actions again sliding up and down on his erect member. Within a couple minutes she felt herself release. David felt a warm rush of liquid cascade down on to him as she slowed to a stop upon him. She collapsed down upon him burying her face into his neck.

David laid there for a moment then rolled her over onto her back. The action caused him to slide out from inside her. He grabbed her legs and placed them upon his shoulders Looking down he could see their mixed juices running out and down her. Guiding himself into her he pushed himself in as deep as he could go. She gasped and bit her lower lip as he slammed himself into her. She could feel him hitting her cervix and it felt tremendous. Within mere seconds she was having another powerful orgasm.

David continued his frenzied assault of her womanhood and she was enjoying every thrust. After a couple more minutes she felt David's pace quicken and

then the familiar feeling of him releasing inside her once again. David collapsed against her visibly exhausted. She rolled onto her side as David snuggled up to her back. His wet member pressing again in to the cleft of her backside. She felt his hand come around and rest cupping her breast. It was not long till she heard him sleeping.

Alyson laid there as her overworked muscles started stiffing. She was already sore from the previous evenings events, and the last hour was just going to make it that much worse. She sighed and resigned that she would try a long hot bath later to see if that would help. What weighed on her mind though was the one thing she was certain of, and that was that her past was now directing their future.

CHAPTER 5

It was a typical Wednesday at school David was excited like he was almost everyday cause he got to see Molly in fourth period science. Then they usually had lunch together afterwards. Science was one of David's favorite classes. He enjoyed the whole discovery aspect of it. Learning the why's and how's of how everything works was intriguing to him. Looking through microscopes at things you couldn't see with your naked eye was an experience he couldn't describe.

David and Molly ended up getting paired up as lab partners. She was reading the lab manual while David was looking through the microscope at the slide.

"You have plans this weekend?" Molly whispered into his ear.

"Not yet, but things could change." David replied not taking his eye from the microscope. "Why, do you have

plans?"

"No, I thought maybe we could do something." She said.

"Sure like what?" David asked.

"Maybe have dinner Friday night?" Molly continued still looking at the lab manual in front of her.

"Sure where would you like to go?" David queried stepping aside so Molly could use the microscope.

"I was thinking maybe you could come to my house." Molly offered as she looked through the microscope.

David grabbed the next slide and started preparing it. When Molly finished looking she turned to face David as she waited his response.

"Dinner with your parents? I thought you were talking just the two of us." He claimed "Sure that sounds like a lot of fun why not." He added sarcastically as he swapped the slides in the microscope. Then returned to looking through it.

Molly placed her mouth close to his ear and said in a soft whisper. "My parents are going to be out of town. We will have the house all to ourselves." David completely forgot about what he was doing and turned to look at her. He saw a mischievous look in her eye and a devilish grin on her face. Then as quickly as it appeared it vanished.

"Come on now, we have to get this done." Molly said

pushing David back towards where the microscope was sitting. David's thoughts were no longer anywhere near science class.

David was sitting waiting for his sisters at his usual spot. He didn't really like going to private school but his mother insisted. He checked his watch and it was 4:15 He hopped down from the wall he was sitting on and started walking towards home. Almost like clockwork his sister came rolling up next to him.

"Sorry were late, It was my fault." Tina stated as she got out of the front seat and gave David a hug. "I got detention for being late to class after lunch."

"You mean late again!" Danni added. "Now get in the car before you make me late for work." She growled. David headed for the back seat.

"You can have the front seat." Tina offered.

"It's OK." David said as he slid into the back seat. Tina followed right behind him, as Danni drove off down the street.

"I have inventory tonight at work so I won't be home till probably midnight." Danni started. "Mom is out of town for work so you and Tina are on your own tonight." David just rolled his eyes at Tina as Danni kept talking. "Mom left some money if you want to get something for

dinner or you can cook something." She continued. Tina pinched her fingers and thumb together several times as Danni spoke. Cleverly doing it so that David could see it but Danni would not.

"We know Danni." David finally said "It's not like we haven't had to do this before."

"I know but it's the first time Mom is out of town leaving us alone." Danni rebuked "You know how much she worries. It's different than if she was just going to be home late." She continued.

David knew it was just Danni stepping up to the role of mother whether she needed to or not.

"OK we got it, no wild parties, no drugs, and no sex." Tina said mockingly as she leaned against David.

"Exactly no fun what so ever." David quickly added with a smirk on his face.

"OK so we all understand each other." Danni said as she turned the car into the driveway.

The three got out and went into the house. David went to his room and laid down on his bed. A few minutes later he heard Danni say goodbye as she walked out the door.

"No homework tonight?" Tina asked standing in the doorway of David's room.

"Nope, I got it all done during study hall. It's nice that it is my last class of the day." David said as he propped

himself up on his elbows. "What about you?"

"Same, I got it all done at school too." Tina replied. "I think I'm gonna go take a shower." She said turning around. "Go ahead and order a pizza for dinner ok?" Tina added as she walked down the hall towards the bathroom. "unless you want to join me?" She joked, or at least David thought she was joking.

Forty five minutes later David was sitting at the table with two bowls of green salad and a Large Meat Lovers pizza sitting on it.

"Tina dinner is here." He yelled down the hall.

"OK be right there" She yelled back.

David had turned to see his sister walking down the hall. She was wearing a blue and white checkered button up shirt with pearl snap buttons. She tied the bottom in a knot so it was tight around her waist. She was wearing a pair of blue jeans and was walking bare foot.

"What do you think? Tomorrow is western day at school and I thought I would wear this." Tina inquired as David stood there staring at her outfit.

"Uh you might want to wear shoes. But other than that it looks good." David said as he turned and walked over to the table.

"Well obviously, I wanted to borrow your cowboy

boots D. Is that ok?" She asked as she followed him over to the table.

"Sure, you don't need to ask though you can just wear them." He said. "Besides I think you know more about what's in my closet than I do." He added.

"Well our closets are joined together." Tina said smiling as she took a bite of her pizza. David just laughed and took a bite of his pizza. They continued their back and forth banter about this and that as they ate dinner. As they talked David couldn't help but notice that Tina's shirt was unbuttoned a little bit lower than was normal for her. As she moved he would get little glimpses of her light blue bra from the opening.

Once dinner was finished Tina jumped up and cleared the table leaving David just sitting there. "Since you cooked, I'll do the dishes." She said.

"Like that's hard it's just two bowls, two glasses and an empty pizza box." David retorted with a smirk on his face. Tina placed the dishes in the dishwasher and turned back to the dining room. David was standing next to the table just watching his sister in the kitchen.

"So what is going through that brain of yours D?" Tina inquired as he just stood there. David just shrugged his shoulders but said nothing. Tina walked towards him with a little grin on her face and a playful sparkle in her eye.

David stood his ground as she got closer to him. Once they were face to face she reached out and wrapped her arms around him and gave him a big hug. Then without warning she gave him a kiss on the lips and pushed her tongue into his mouth.

It was similar to the kiss she had given him before they left on the ski trip last month. But this time instead of a quick kiss this one lasted longer.

"What was that for?" David asked his sister still hugging him tightly.

"Just for being you. You are really the best brother a sister could ask for." Tina said as she released her grip.

"Well I'm not really that special. I have a lot of flaws. Besides you're a pretty great sister if my opinion counts." David countered.

"Ah, that's so sweet D. But I think maybe your just buttering me up so you can see my bra again." Tina winked. "I saw you stealing glances at it all throughout dinner." She added.

"Well If you would learn how to button your shirt that wouldn't have happened." David replied with a slight grin on his face. They stood there staring at each other in complete silence for an awkward few moments. Finally Tina erupted in laughter with David quickly following her. They laughed for what seemed like five minutes. When

they finished Tina had a serious look on her face once again.

"Ok well I'm gonna go change out of this now." She said as she turned and headed towards her bedroom. David watched her butt swing as she walked down the hall.

"Can I ask you something?" David called out before he could stop himself.

"Sure Anything you know that." She answered.

"Remember when you said to let you know if I changed my mind about seeing your breasts?" David continued.

"Yea I think I remember that." Tina responded slightly surprised.

"Well I think I changed my mind." David said coyly.

"Oh, OK, well come on then." Tina said as she waved her arm in a motion that indicated him to follow her as she turned into her bedroom. David followed down the hall and entered into the room behind her. "Only one condition, You have to remove my clothes." Tina stated as David entered the room.

"Are you sure?" David inquired.

"Yea that's my rules." Tina said just standing there waiting to see what David was going to do.

David stepped up behind his sister and reached his arms around her and untied the knot at the bottom of her

shirt. Then reached up towards the neck grasping each half of the open shirt in each hand. In one quick motion he pulled his arms apart and the button snaps of the shirt gave way quickly and effortlessly. Within a few seconds Tina was standing there with her shirt laying on the floor.

Tina turned to face David with a surprised look on her face.

"Well that was kind of forceful. Are you a little excited?" Tina said with a smile.

"Maybe a little bit." David said as he reached his arms around her back following the bra strap. As David's hands fumbled around looking for the clasp. He got a puzzled look on his face when he couldn't find it. Tina laughed as David continued his search.

"It's in the front genius" Tina said mockingly.

David leaned back slightly and looking down he found the clasp and studied it briefly before attempting to unfasten it. Once the clasp was released her breasts burst from her bra like an overstuffed piñata. In a moment her bra was lying next to the shirt on the floor.

David stood there just admiring them. He wanted to touch them but wasn't sure if he should. Then Tina grabbed his hand and placed it on one of her breasts.

"It's ok if you want to touch them." She said as she stood there.

David moved so he was standing behind her once again and reached around so that both hands were cupping each of her breasts. Her skin was soft and supple and her breasts were firm. Her nipples were now erect and responding to his manipulation of them. Tina reached back and pulled David against her.

"Is that all you want to see?" Tina inquired. David lowered his hands to the waist line of her jeans. His hands found the closure then stopped. "It's ok, Continue if you want too." Tina added.

David gave a tug and the button came apart easily. Then he unzipped them and pulled them down over her hips. In moments they joined her shirt and bra on the floor. David's hands returned to her waist looking for her panties and found that she was not wearing any.

"My turn." Tina stated as she turned around and pulled David's T-shirt up over his head. She had his pants and underwear off in quick succession as well. Within moments both of them were standing in the middle of her bedroom completely naked. David stood there studying Tina's body in the light. As his gaze traveled down her body he stopped when he reached her pubic area and found that she only had a small strip of hair just above it.

Tina grabbed David's hand a pulled him over to her bed. The two of them fell onto the bed and snuggled up

next to each other. David was confused by this interaction but was enjoying it. Tina reached down and grabbed his throbbing member in her hand and started stroking it. David in return started to kiss her breasts and sucked on her nipples.

Tina was enjoying the feeling of David's touch and kisses on her breasts. So much so that she forgot that this was her first sexual experience with anyone. She pushed David over onto his back and straddled him. She felt his hard member pressing against her backside. David laid there wondering what she was thinking. After a few moments he pulled Tina down to him and held her against his chest. The feeling of their bare chests touching was wonderful. David slid his hand down between her legs and searched for the warm spot.

Seconds later Tina felt a tingle travel up her spine as David found her clitoris and started rubbing it. Startled she pulled away from him.

"Sorry, I thought you were enjoying this." David said with a look of remorse.

"I am, It's just this is my first time." Tina confessed. "I just wanted it to be with someone I trust." She paused then continued. "There is no one I trust more than you." Tina finished.

"I understand." David said as he pulled her close to

him and kissed her neck. David and Tina laid in bed just holding each other for the next half hour.

Tina grabbed ahold of David's still ridged member a second time. As she stroked it she could feel it growing in her hand. David massaged and sucked on her breasts as he rolled her onto her back. He softly kissed down her chest and down to her belly. He continued further down till he found his way to her smooth mound. He licked her sweet juices then shoved his tongue deep inside her fold.

"Oh my" Tina's voice cried out as her back arched and her legs tightened against David's head. Without giving away any ground David grabbed her hips and drove his face and tongue deeper inside her. Tina's hands dug into the sheets as the waves of pleasure cascaded over her. In a few short minutes she was surprised as she achieved an orgasm from David's oral assault.

David returned to kissing up her torso till he reached her chest again. Tina was breathing heavy and holding on to his arms shaking. He felt her spread her legs apart as he searched for the right spot. He found it and started to push himself inside her. Even though she had already had one orgasm it was very tight. David could barely get the head of his tool inside her. As he added a little more force Tina let out a loud scream that froze David in place.

"I'm sorry." David said with a concerned look on his

face.

"It's ok, Don't stop, Just keep going." Tina breathlessly said staring back into David's eyes. "They said the first time could be a little painful in health class at school." She added.

David nodded and proceeded to push himself further into her. After another painful scream emitted from Tina's lips he felt himself reach total depth. The pair just laid there joined together.

"What's wrong?" Tina finally asked as she looked at her brother.

"I'm afraid that I'm hurting you." David exclaimed.

"Well I won't lie. It does hurt a little bit. But I know you aren't meaning to hurt me and I am still enjoying it. Besides I think the worst of it is over." Tina replied giving David a little wink.

Unbeknownst to David, Tina had been researching everything she could find about her first sexual experience for months. This wasn't planned but she wasn't about to pass up this opportunity either.

David was surprised at just how much tighter she was compared to his mother but the feeling was almost the same; he delivered a few strokes and it seemed that Tina just got wetter as he moved inside her. David felt her wrap her legs up around his waist as he fell into a slow rhythm.

It seemed like just a matter of seconds before she was so moist that he was sliding in and out of her with little effort. Occasionally Tina would utter a few vocalizations of pleasure, accompanied by a pained tone. But she continued to hold on to David tightly. After another five minutes David felt his sister release a massive orgasm. As her warm juices cascaded over him he exploded inside her as well.

Tina released the death grip she had on David as if every ounce of her strength had been instantly zapped away. David collapsed onto the bed beside her both breathing heavy and lying motionless. They laid there for several minutes in silence just staring at the ceiling.

David's mind was a rush of confusion and pleasure. He wasn't sure how this had happened but he wasn't complaining about it either. He had half expected his sister to back out shortly after he got her naked, but he was caught off guard by her removing his clothes in turn. One thing was for sure this was a totally different experience than what he shared with his mother.

"What you thinking about D?" Tina asked now laying on her side with her head propped up on her hand.

"Oh nothing really, my mind is a blank slate." David responded as he turned on his side to face her. Tina ran her hand down David's chest and abdomen stopping just

shy of his package and traced her way back up.

"Did you enjoy it?" She inquired trying to avoid eye contact for the moment.

"Uh yea I did, you kind of surprised me though. I wasn't expecting anything like that." David said as the words tumbled from his mouth and his eyes scanned down his sisters body mentally recording everything.

"Oh well, we still have at least four hours before Danni will be home. You think you might want to go again?" Tina quizzed with that devilish look in her eye.

"Sure if you do." David didn't even have to think about it he was willing to do anything his sister asked at that point. "But shouldn't we be using protection or something?" He asked almost as an afterthought.

Tina met his gaze with hers as the words left David's lips. "Don't worry about that D. I've been on the pill for a couple months. Everything is taken care of." She finally stated as she pushed him onto his back.

"Besides I think he's ready for round two don't you?" Tina said pointing at David's swollen member.

David just nodded his agreement as Tina lowered herself down onto it slowly as she allowed it to fully fill her up. David watched as a pained look crossed her face for a moment then quickly passed. Slowly at first she started riding up and down on him as David just watched her.

David reached up and put his hands on her hips as she continued to bounce on top of him. Softly at first noises of pleasure escaped her mouth and continued to grow louder. Tina was making sure she was using every bit of his manhood as she would slide up to the top till he almost came out of her and then drop back down onto him. The pleasure was worth the small amount of pain it was causing.

After several more repetitions of this maneuver Tina's moaning grew louder then morphed into a scream. David felt the sudden onslaught of wetness crash upon him as she reached her climax. Almost simultaneously David erupted in an orgasm of his own. Tina slowed her bouncing and came to a stop as David bent up and wrapped his arms around her torso. His mouth came to the exact height of her beautiful breasts and he instantly took it into his mouth gently sucking on the nipple and holding her tight against him.

He dropped his hand down till he felt her smooth round buttocks and grabbed a big handful and squeezed.

"Oh damn D, not so hard." Tina giggled. David just bit down slightly on her nipple and pulled back stretching it. Then he slapped her butt with his hand. Then in a move that surprised Tina. He quickly flipped her over on the bed ensuring that she landed prone on the mattress.

He grabbed her hips and pulled them up till she got her knees under her and moved himself behind her.

Without warning David drove himself deep inside her moist wet hole. Tina's head shot back in surprised shock as David slammed his pelvis into hers. Grabbing a hold of her hips he pulled out almost completely and slammed it back in deep and hard. Tina let out a painful scream as David drove his full girth home.

"Oh my god, D don't you dare stop." Tina hollered in pleasure filled pain.

David just tightened his grip on her hips and repeated the same maneuver. Each subsequent thrust was deeper and harder than the previous one. David's fingers dug deeper into her flesh as he continued his feverous assault of her body. Each thrust was a mix of pleasure and pain for Tina. Her hips were starting to burn from David's grip getting increasingly tighter. She buried her face in her pillow half of her wishing he would stop, and half of her wishing it would never end. Nothing in her research even mentioned this position or the feelings it was causing within her.

After a couple moments she reached another orgasm which was quickly followed by another and then another. She expected David to be tiring out but he was delivering the same intensity as before. She felt herself growing faint

and thought she would pass out at any minute. Finally with one particularly hard thrust she felt David explode inside her. David relaxed his grip on her hips and Tina crumpled to the bed in a heap with David crashing down on top of her.

David laid there on top of his sister panting trying to catch his breath. Tina laid motionless underneath her brother attempting to catch her breath as well. She could feel their combined juices draining out from inside her. She could feel her muscles stiffening as she rested. This was definitely nowhere near what she expected sex to be like. She shifted slightly and felt David roll off of her. She turned over and laid on her back next to David.

"Well that was wonderful D" she finally managed to speak. "I hope you enjoyed it as well." She added.

"Yes I enjoyed that a lot." David replied as he pulled her close to him. "I really wasn't expecting this. I have to say I'm quite surprised."

"Why?" Tina asked confused by David's reply.

"Well I mean it not what you expect to do with your sister for one." David said.

"Oh, I see." Tina said with a hint of pain in her voice. "It's just I wanted to have my first time be with someone I love and trust." She continued. "I really love you David and I thought that you would want to share this with me as

well."

"Well I do love you Tina, your my sister and always will be. Your very important to me." David said. "I just didn't expect it is all." David took Tina's hand in his. "It just kind of confusing is all. But I really enjoyed sharing this experience with you." David added hoping he was putting her at ease.

Tina sat up on the edge of the bed while David laid there. Finally after a few moments she stood up and turned around and faced David. Her legs felt like jelly and all of the muscles in her pubic area were screaming. She looked down at the bed that was completely soaked in fluid from their extensive session.

"Well I think I need a shower." Tina said as she started to leave the room. " You probably should take one too; Or you can just join me." She added as she disappeared from his sight.

David jumped to his feet and grabbed his clothes as he followed her out the door. He tossed them into the hamper in his room and crossed the hall to the bathroom. Tina already had the shower turned on and heating up. David stepped up behind her and put his arms around her. Tina could feel his slightly erect penis pressing against her backside.

"Wow you must have really enjoyed it if you are getting

hard again D." Tina stated.

"Yea I could go again. You felt really good." David said not loosening his grip.

"Well I don't know if I could handle another session like that right now. But maybe we can do it again sometime." Tina said as she moved towards the shower.

"Anytime you want." David answered as he followed her into the shower.

The hot water washed over the two of them rinsing the fluids off of their bodies. Looking down David noticed a little bit of blood running down Tina's leg and continuing down the drain.

"I'm sorry Tina, your bleeding. Did I hurt you?" David asked alarmed.

"Oh no D." she replied seeing the blood as well. "It's just sometimes for females that are virgins there is some tearing and a little bit of bleeding. It's completely normal." Tina said as she lathered up her body.

"OK well I know I got a little carried away. I just wanted you to know I wasn't trying to hurt you." David said sheepishly.

Tina turned around and kissed David while she pushed him against the wall.

"Your cute." Tina quipped as she kneeled down in front of him and started kissing his hard cock. Then she

took it into her mouth. David just leaned against the wall enjoying the impromptu blow job his sister was now giving him.

After several minutes David reached climax and burst into Tina's mouth. She coughed a couple times but swallowed every ounce that he emitted. Afterward She stood up and continued her shower as David just stood there and watched her.

Tina then turned around and washed David as he just stood there admiring her beautiful body. Once they finished with their shower David returned to his room and climbed into bed. About a half hour later Tina came through the closet and was standing next to his bed. Without asking she climbed in bed with David and snuggled up next to him.

"My bed is wet, I'm going to sleep with you tonight." Tina whispered. David rolled over and snuggled up to her back and put his arm over her. Slowly he slid his hand under her t-shirt till he found her breast. Cupping it in his hand he quickly drifted off to sleep.

CHAPTER 6

It was about two weeks ago when Molly had a gymnastics meet on Saturday. David was excited to go not because he liked gymnastics but mostly just to see Molly do what she enjoyed doing. David sat in the bleachers and was positive Molly was unable to pick him out in the crowd of people. The meet lasted a little over three hours, to David it seemed like it was a lot longer than that. But he stayed through the whole thing cheering for her during her routines.

It was Molly's second attempt at the vault. Her first vault was almost perfect. She had scored a 8.92 and was sitting solidly in second place. Molly approached the runway and prepared for her second run. Even if she performed a low difficulty vault she would have remained in second place. David could see the determination on her face.

Molly burst forward and quickly hit her full speed as she ran down the runway. Molly executed a forward

handspring onto the springboard. She launched up into the air as her hands hit the vault platform. Molly twisted and turned as she somersaulted through the air. When Molly's feet hit the mat she seemed to be of balance. Through sheer will Molly forced her body to stick the landing. But it was at a cost as her ankle rolled out from underneath her. Molly managed to not show the injury and walked off the mat as a single tear ran down her face.

David wanted to fly out of the stands and run to Molly, but he stayed put. Molly's coach half walked half carried her into the locker room. David felt sick inside he didn't know how bad Molly had gotten hurt. As the rest of the gymnasts continued their routines David's mind ran wild. Finally the meet concluded and Molly's scores secured her a second place finish. As people started filing out of the gymnasium David remained seated. Once everyone had left and Molly still hadn't come out. David made his way outside to wait for Molly.

It was about an hour later when Molly emerged walking on what looked like a very painful ankle. David couldn't help but smile as she slowly limped over towards him. As she got closer to David she started smiling too. Once she reached him she collapsed into his arms.

"I'm glad you came." Molly said as she hugged David.

"I told you I would be here. I figured you wouldn't be

able to spot me among all the other people in there." David replied just holding Molly tight against his chest.

"Of course I saw you. You didn't think I wouldn't be able to spot my boyfriend did you?" Molly asked looking into David's eyes.

"Does your ankle hurt?" David quickly attempted to change the subject.

"Oh just a little, It's not the first time I have sprained my ankle. I sure it won't be my last." Molly laughed.

David opened the car door and let Molly slide into the passenger seat. He shut the door and walked around to the driver's side and got in. as he started the car Molly cuddled up to his arm and they pulled out of the parking lot.

It was strange that Molly's parents hadn't been at the meet to begin with as they regularly attended all of them. She said that her father had some kind of business lunch and they both had to be there. The funny thing was Molly felt more at ease without them there than she ever had with them there.

Molly's parents would have gone ballistic had they found out David was driving Molly back from the gymnastics meet. The meet was only an hour drive from their home. Apparently that was further than they were comfortable with him driving their daughter home. But they had lightened up enough to let him drive her around

town. So he really couldn't complain too much.

The entire drive back Molly just laid her head on David's arm. When David turned onto her street he wanted to just keep driving right past her house and down the road. David pulled into the driveway and got out of the car and walked around to help Molly out of the car. He helped her to the door and into the house. Seizing the opportunity he gave Molly a big kiss once they got inside the door. Molly kissed him back and then pushed him away.

"My parents will be coming home soon and I don't want to hear another lecture about how I am not supposed to be riding with you in a car when you have only had your license for a few months." Molly said as she pushed David out the door.

"Ok, I guess I will see you at school on Monday then?" David asked as he headed for the car.

"Yes, Or maybe we can chat or skype online later." Molly said as she watched him walk away.

David climbed in the car and drove away as Molly disappeared behind the closing front door. He almost hated how over bearing Molly's parents were. But he also knew there was nothing he could about it either. David made a few turns and then headed in out of Molly's neighborhood. He noticed Molly's parents car pass but

they didn't seem to recognize them. When David got home he pulled the car into the garage and parked it next to Tina's car.

It was one of the few things that his mother had managed to keep after his father's death. Danni, Tina, and David each had their own cars. David's father had made a great deal with a friend of his who owned a car dealership. He had gotten a deal on some low mileage repossessions. The cars were not that great by some standards but they were better than most. Danni being the oldest and having her license first got first choice. Danni chose the red 2000 Chevrolet Malibu, Since Tina was the second oldest she got to choose next and she decided the blue 2000 Volkswagen Jetta was the car for her. That left David with the black 2002 Ford Escort. It wasn't flashy or sporty but it ran and was a safe car.

David walked in the house and headed towards his bedroom. He hadn't heard any sounds of life so he figured that he had the house to himself. He decided to change his clothes and go for a short run since he had to skip his morning run to go to the gymnastics meet. David striped down to his underwear and grabbed his shorts and t-shirt. He laced up his shoes and grabbed his MP3 player as he headed out the door.

His run took him through the wooded area of Mill

Creek and then up onto the Mountain side that skirted the neighborhood below. He finished his run on the far end of the development and then headed back towards his house. As what usually happened his favorite song would start playing on his MP3 player just as he would be getting home.

David entered the house and found it to be empty and just as quiet as before. Danni was most likely at work which was normal for a Saturday. He walked into the kitchen and found a note sitting on the counter.

David-

Went to the movies with Sally and Jeff then going to go have dinner. Won't be home till after 10, Danni is working a double so she won't be home either. You and Tina will have to fend for yourselves.

Love Mom

David crumpled note and tossed it into the garbage can and turned around and headed to his room. He changed into his sweats and threw his running clothes into his clothes hamper. He walked back out to the kitchen and made himself a grilled cheese sandwich and returned to his

room and laid down on his bed and turned on his TV. About an hour later David heard someone come in the door of the house. In a moment Tina was standing in the doorway of David's room. Tina was dressed in a navy blue baggy t-shirt and a pair of black yoga pants. It was Tina's usual comfy outfit that she wore on weekends. David just laid there watching TV. Tina walked over and dropped down onto the bed. She grabbed the fleece blanket on the end of the bed and covered herself with it and snuggled up next to David.

"Is this ok?" Tina asked as she laid her head on his shoulder.

"Yea it's fine." David replied as he put his arm around her shoulders. The two of them didn't say another word to each other the rest of the night but just laid on the bed and watched TV.

All day long Friday David's mind was anywhere but on school work. He was feeling in really good spirits. Even the school Psychiatrist even commented on David's change in attitude at his monthly session.

David sat across the desk from the Psychiatrist in her office. As she looked over his records. Then she laid the folder down on the desk.

"David It looks like your grades are improving in all your classes finally. If this trend continues you will be able to get back into your advanced placement classes when school resumes after Christmas break." She said as she stared at David. "So what is behind this turn around?" She inquired.

"Well I guess I just got tired of feeling sorry for myself. I couldn't change what happened so I decided that I had to live my life." David paused. "Oh and I got a girlfriend too." He added as an afterthought.

The psychiatrist just smiled and wrote some notes on her notepad. As they continued their conversation David noticed that she was writing less and less on the notepad. He figured that had to be a good thing since in most of his other sessions with her he thought she was writing a novel about him.

At the end of their session she told him they would meet next month just before break and would discuss his being placed back into his advanced placement classes. David walked down the hall towards his science class eager to see Molly. As he got to the door of the classroom the bell rang and the class was emptying out. Molly walked out the door and grabbed David's hand as they walked down to the cafeteria.

They picked up their trays and walked through the line

and got their lunch and went over to a table and sat down.

"Your still coming over tonight right?" Molly asked as she ate her salad.

"There is nothing that would keep me away." David replied. "Besides I've been wanting to spend some alone time with you for a while now." He added. "It always seems like your parents are always around when we have time to spend together. I can't even kiss you in front of them." David stated as he took a bite of his salad.

"Well you can kiss me all you want tonight. Or whatever else that might enter that mind of yours." Molly teased David. "My parents left for Los Angeles this morning and won't be home till Sunday night. So we will have the house all to ourselves." Molly added.

"That sounds nice; being able to be alone with you." David said as he continued to eat his lunch. Molly pulled her phone out of her pocket and tapped the screen a couple times and then placed it on the table and slid it over to David.

"And If you're lucky you might get to see me in this later." Molly whispered.

David looked down at the phone and choked on the bite of food in his mouth. The picture on Molly's phone was a selfie of her in a skimpy navy blue bikini that tied on the sides. The picture was very revealing and very out of

character of the image Molly portrayed to everyone else.

Molly just laughed as she watched David's eyes almost pop right out of his head. Then she reached down and grabbed her phone before anyone else could see the picture.

"I thought I might wear that while we relax in the hot tub tonight." She continued. "It's a lot more comfortable than the one piece speedo suit I wear for diving." She stated. "I knew you would like it."

"Yea, I like it a lot. I am looking forward to seeing it on you tonight." David said with a smile on his face. David wanted to kiss Molly right at that moment, but the schools code of conduct about public displays of affection prevented it. He reached out and squeezed her hand the two continued their lunch chatting about various topics.

To say David was walking on cloud nine for the rest of the day would have been an understatement. He was in such a great mood he didn't' even mind going to 5th period English class. English was by far his weakest subject and yet he had gotten his grade up to a high B. That was a feat in itself since for as far back as he could remember he could barely get it above a C. All the hard work was paying off he thought to himself. The truth was that it was the hours of tutoring he was getting from Molly.

They would meet at the library in town on Thursdays after school. Molly would then tutor him for an hour sometimes two. The library had three private rooms that students could use for group projects and tutoring sessions. The two of them had the room booked every Thursday for the last couple months.

David enjoyed the private time with Molly. Away from school they could hold hands, kiss, and hug each other. Things they weren't allowed to do at school, with the exception of hold hands. The privacy they found at the library enabled them to be cute, and comfortable with each other. The library was just one small part of being able to be alone together.

Other than their time at the library the only time they had to be alone together was their Saturday morning runs. David was a long distance runner. He had won several medals in Track and Field. He also liked the fact that running also helped with his swimming. Besides improving his endurance it also kept his legs strong. He really enjoyed running as he found it was the only time he could be alone with his thoughts.

Even though he and Molly ran together every Saturday he still had that alone time to be with his thoughts. Molly was also an accomplished long distance runner in her own right. She like him had also won several track medals and

117

awards.

Molly had been in gymnastics since she was five years old. She started diving when she was ten because the two sports complimented each other. Molly's mother Heather had been a gymnast herself and had almost made it to the Olympics. Due to an unfortunate accident though she was never able to achieve her dream. Molly always felt that her mother's unattained dream was the reason she pushed Molly so hard.

Molly couldn't remember a time when she had ever been able to just relax and be who she wanted to be. She was getting tired of her mother living vicariously through her. When she wanted to start diving her mother did everything she could to dissuade her from it. It wasn't till her diving couch and gymnastic coach both agreed that it would improve her gymnastics performance.

Molly had hoped her skill in diving would outshine her gymnastic abilities. That way she would be able to break free from pursuing her mother's dreams. She had even tried to get her father to get her mother to lighten up, but that just made things worse. When he did try to get her mother to loosen up it would just lead to them fighting.

Molly just felt like her mother was controlling every facet of her life. She was excited when they enrolled her into the private school because it had one of the best

diving and swimming programs in the state. She felt her parents were to controlling but eventually resigned to just live with it.

That was until she saw David walk into school that first day. From the first day she saw him she was hooked. He was tall and very good looking. He had a mysterious dark side to him that just made him even more appealing. She tried everything she could think of to get him to notice her. But he just seemed to be locked in his own little world. That was until that day they ran into each other on their morning run.

Things changed between them that day. Little by little David slowly emerged from his shell. It took a little bit of prodding from Molly but he slowly started to come around. Molly had even changed her class schedule so that she and David would have science class together. Molly had wanted to change all her classes so she could be in the same classes together but the school wouldn't allow it. After that they started talking more and within a week or two they were having lunch together.

Molly's parents on the other hand were a different story altogether. After repeatedly asking, her parents reluctantly allowed David to take her out to dinner once or twice. After that almost anytime they got to spend together outside of school was usually in the company of her

parents. Her parents were somewhat strict and that made it hard for her and David to have any time alone together.

Even when her parents let them sit watch movies in the theater room down stairs. All they could do was hold hands and snuggle together a little. David would not even attempt to give her a kiss when her parents were around. Their Saturday morning run quickly became their favorite part of the week. It was just them alone and the wooded trails that they started running on served two purposes. One to offer them privacy they both sought and the added difficulty of trail running enhanced their running abilities.

Even with running seven to ten miles on trails together they never really had the privacy they had hoped for. Once while on their run they stopped at a small clearing. While they sat taking a rest they got a little carried away kissing. Neither one of them realized when a couple of their classmates came walking through the clearing a little bit later. Molly was so startled she screamed right in David's ear. After that incident Molly and David rarely shared anything more than kisses while running. She was too scared that someone might see them and tell her parents or worse her parents might come looking for her and catch her and David.

David didn't think it was a big deal. The trails that covered the wilderness park that they ran at were so

numerous that they never ran the same trail twice. But the thought of her being grounded and them not getting to see each other was enough of a deterrent for David to keep his emotions in check. Besides he still had the time at the library where they were alone and no one knew where they were.

Both David and Molly kept the private library tutoring and study sessions a secret. David hadn't even shared it with his most trusted confidant, his sister Tina. It wasn't really a secret but they both agreed that the fewer people that knew about it the better it was for the both of them.

Before David knew it English was over and it was time for sixth period study hall. It wasn't really a class but more of a free period. Students were allowed to actually leave school after their fifth period class to attend sports practices and other school activities. Since the school rules dictated that only seniors could drive personal vehicles to school. David was unable to leave the school even if he wanted to.

Like most of the students that had the luxury of the free sixth period class but couldn't leave school. David used it as study hall. Sometimes he would actually do school work but most of the time he would just sit and day dream.

Today however was not one of those days. David

121

found a seat at one of the tables toward the back of the room and spread his books out on top of it. David was one of four Juniors at school that had the luxury of the free sixth period. All of them like him were advanced placement students. Just like him they had all met the state mandate for required learning. Two of them used the free period to take first year college classes. To get a leg up on college when they graduated. David had planned to do the same after winter break but for now the added homework time was more than welcome.

The rest of the students filed into the class room and spread out. Within minutes the 14 total students were quietly doing homework or looking at their tablets and cell phones. David hurried through his chemistry homework and then started on the only other homework for the weekend and that was calculus. After about twenty minutes he finished and closed his book. Looking up at the clock he saw he still had about ten minutes till class was over.

Once the bell rang David walked to his locker and placed all his books inside and closed the door. He threw his empty backpack over his left shoulder and headed to the usual pick up spot in front of the school. To David's surprise his sisters were sitting in front of the school waiting for him.

"Well this is a change." David smirked. "Usually I'm waiting for you two." He added with a playful grin on his face.

"Shut up D!" David's sisters replied in perfect unison. Tina just pushed him into the back seat and climbed in after him. The trio rode in silence back to the house.

"Seems strange for you not to have homework David" Danni said as they got out of the car.

" Yea I got it all done at school. Guess I was just extra motivated today." He stated.

Danni just looked at him over her shoulder and shrugged. She thought it was strange since David usually had homework every weekend. But then again he seemed to be emerging from his protective cocoon that he had hid in after their father's death so she wasn't complaining. Danni walked up the walk ahead of David and Tina.

Danni had her long dark brown hair pulled back into a pony tail and was wearing a pink and white striped knit shirt and a pair of white linen pants. Since one of David's chores was to do the laundry he knew that Danni's wore a size 10 pant. But he never recalled having washed those particular pants before. The material was fairly thin and he could easily make out the fact that Danni was not wearing any underwear underneath her pants as he couldn't detect any presence of a panty line.

"You stare any harder and they might catch fire." Tina whispered into David's ear as they got to the door of the house. David turned and looked at his sister. She just smiled and walked through the door ahead of him.

David walked to his room and dropped his backpack on the floor. He laid down on his bed and stared up at the ceiling. His mind was a jumble of thoughts about what the coming evening would hold for him. After several minutes he headed for the shower to get ready.

David stood with a towel wrapped around his waist just staring into his closet. It wasn't particularly hard to decide what he should wear he just wasn't sure if it was going to be a jeans night or if something a little more formal was required. He finally settled on a pair of black slacks and a light blue button up shirt.

As he turned around to get dressed his towel fell to the floor.

"Well that's some pretty impressive equipment there. You might want to close the door once in a while." Danni said as she passed David's room. David's face turned red as he quickly crossed the room and swung the door closed. He heard the front door open then close and Danni start her car and drive off. David was shocked to say the least but just shrugged it off. He resumed dressing and put the encounter out of his mind.

Tina was sitting in the living room and overheard Danni's comment as she walked down the hall. Tina had just looked at her sister with disbelief on her face. Danni just looked back at her as she winked, at the same time she held her hands apart indicating to her sister the size It was so out of character for Danni to say anything let alone call her brother out like that.

Tina already had firsthand knowledge of just how impressive her brother was. She just remained seated on the couch not really watching the program that was on the television. Her mind wandered back to that night. It wasn't something she had planned, it was more of something that just happened. A fortunate string of events that led to their inevitable outcome.

She would never deny that she had considered her brother for her first time. She had always heard and believed that the first time should be with someone you truly love. For her there was no one in her life that she loved more than David. Despite being eleven months apart they had a bond that kept them close.

She wasn't sure how far David would take it that night. She didn't even think he would have got past just looking at her chest. She was certainly just as surprised as he was. Sharing something as personal as that with her brother had just made their bond that much stronger. Tina's mind

wandered back to that night like it had done numerous times before.

She let her mind wander through the events of that night like it was a movie playing in the theater. She could feel his touch and even in her memories her body was still reacting. Her mind trailed on to his kisses and how he enjoyed every inch of her body.

"Tina, Tina, I'm leaving now." David's voice brought her out of her daydream. She opened her eyes to see David standing in front of her.

"Oh, OK have a good night." She replied with a slightly surprised look on her face. David bent down and gave his sister a kiss on the cheek and a hug. Tina wrapped her arms around David and hugged him back.

"Let me fix that." She said as she untied his tie and retied it. "I swear you are gonna have to learn how to tie a tie someday. I'm not always gonna be around to do it for you." Once she finished she grasped the tie and pulled him into her. Then she pressed her lips to his and pushed her tongue into his mouth. David just accepted the kiss and returned in kind. After several moments they stopped kissing and Tina relaxed her grip on David.

"I told you that's how you kiss a woman goodbye. Glad you paid attention." She said as David stood up. "Hope you have a good night D." she added as he headed towards

the door.

"You too. You gonna to be ok home alone?" David said mockingly.

"Yea I don't have any big plans just gonna to camp out on the couch and watch the TV." Tina replied smiling as she watched David disappear behind the closing door.

Tina resumed watching the show on the TV. She was not even sure what was happening on the show since her mind was obviously somewhere else. She closed her eyes again and resumed her day dreaming. After several minutes she realized that she was completely drenched and headed to take a long shower.

CHAPTER 7

David pulled his car into the drive way of Molly's house about a half hour later. He grabbed a bunch of flowers he had picked up at the florist prior to arriving at Molly's house. He walked up to the door and before he could ring the doorbell Molly threw the door open. She was wearing a tight fitting short black dress. The hem line stopped just short of halfway between her hips and her knees.

Molly reached out and grabbed the flowers with one hand and the front of David's shirt with the other and pulled him through the door. She gave David a big kiss as she kicked the door closed with her leg. David wrapped his arms around her as they kissed. The knowledge of the fact that her parents were miles away and were not going to be back anytime soon. Made it just that much easier for the two of them to relax.

Molly turned around and walked towards the kitchen. "Go ahead and make yourself comfortable, dinner will be

ready in a few minutes." She said over her shoulder. The back of her dress was a deep V-Cut and David could instantly tell she wasn't wearing a bra. He didn't even think it was possible to wear one with a dress like that. The dress was very tight fitting and as Molly walked away he strained to see if she had panties on. After she disappeared into the kitchen David walked into the living room and sat down in the easy chair.

The smell from the kitchen was making his mouth water. The only sounds he heard was the sound of pans and utensils clanking together. In a few minutes it was completely quiet. David wasn't sure what to expect or even if Molly could cook at all, but he knew whatever it was he would eat every last bite. David heard the sound of plates being set down on the table and then Molly calling him to come eat. As he turned the corner into the dining room he saw Molly standing next to the table.

The table was set with two plates from her parents fine china collection. Two crystal glasses and a pair of lit white candles in crystal candle holders. There was a large serving dish with a mountain of spaghetti and a smaller bowl with a tossed green salad.

Molly gave David a big hug and a kiss. David wrapped his arms around her waist and pulled her into him. He hugged her tight while they kissed. After a few moments

David released his grip and Molly pulled back slightly.

"I hope you like it." Molly said "It's my grandmothers recipe, she use to make it for me every time we would visit her house." She continued.

"Well it looks delicious." David smiled. "I'm sure it tastes as good as it looks." He said as he started dishing up his plate. Molly just sat there waiting for David to take a bite. David knew what she was waiting for so he grabbed his fork. Plunging it into the middle of the mound of spaghetti; he twisted it around several times till he had a small ball of noodles, meat and sauce on his fork. David brought it up to his mouth and smelled it as he placed it in his mouth. He started chewing expecting the worst but to his surprise it tasted wonderful.

Molly sat waiting on pins and needles for David's reaction. David just slowly chewed the bite in his mouth fully aware it was causing agonizing seconds of uneasiness for Molly. Finally after several more seconds he swallowed the food in his mouth. He looked at Molly for a moment not saying anything. Then just as he started to see tears welling up in her eyes.

"You know that has got to be the best spaghetti I have ever tasted." He said with a slight smirk on his face. Molly slapped his arm so hard it hurt.

"You made me think it was terrible." She stated while

trying to hold back a laugh. David just smiled and placed another bite in his mouth. He figured it was the safest course of action at the moment. Before long they were eating and laughing as they enjoyed the wonderful meal Molly had prepared.

This was the first obstacle that Molly had passed. Not that she would admit it to David but this was the first time she had attempted to make a meal from scratch. She was able to cook fairly well it was something she had learned from her grandmother. Even so though she was still self-conscious with this being the first time she had cooked for him.

David was genuinely surprised. It wasn't that he didn't think Molly could cook it was just that he had never seen her do it or even talk about doing it. He had expected it to be like the first time Tina tried to cook dinner. The aftermath was that every dish in the house was dirty and the meal was neither fully cooked or edible. David knew better than to compare the two instances but it was hard not too.

After dinner David offered to do the dishes, Molly of course refused to let him do them alone and helped him. Once the dishes were done they sat in the living room and cuddled together on the couch and kissing. After about an hour of making out on the couch and enjoying their newly

found freedom to be themselves.

"Let's go sit in the hot tub" Molly stated as she stood up from the couch.

"oh – uh, Ok but I didn't bring a bathing suit." David sheepishly said as he stood up.

That's ok it's just us you don't really need one." Molly countered as she headed towards her bedroom. "You go take the lid off the tub and I'm going to go change." She winked over her shoulder at David. David just stood there with a dumb little smile on his face watching Molly walk down the hall and disappear into her room.

David walked out the back of the house and turned on the hot tub and proceeded to pull the cover off. He stepped back into the house and undressed laying his clothes on the bench by the sliding glass door that led to the deck area where the hot tub was. David stepped through the door and nakedly walked over to the hot tub and disappeared beneath the water eagerly waiting for Molly to arrive.

Molly appeared at the door wearing the same blue bathing suit she was wearing in the picture she showed David earlier that day. Molly just stood there looking a David who had the same goofy look on his face that he did when she showed him the picture.

"Well I'm glad you like it." Molly stated as she started

crossing the deck to the hot tub. David didn't utter a word he just watched Molly walking towards him. David stood up as Molly stepped into the hot tub. David placed his hands on her hips as she stepped down into the water. As her hips disappeared below the water line David fingers pulled at the ties on either side. Molly watched as her bikini bottom floated up to the surface of the hot tub. Without protesting she continued descending into the hot tub. As she came to sit on the seat next to David her bikini top was joining her bottoms floating on the water's surface.

"Well that didn't stay on long" She smirked.

"I figured that since I was already naked and we were alone there was no reason you shouldn't be naked too." David surmised as he relaxed in the warm water. Molly just grabbed her suit and threw it over by the sliding glass door and laid her head on David's shoulder. After a few minutes she turned her body and placed her legs over David's lap.

David just sat there not sure what he should do next. Molly was confused as to why David hadn't tried to do anything yet. In the past David had tried almost anything he could to get Molly undressed. Not that she minded though. Yet at this moment they were both naked together and he hadn't tried a single thing.

David's mind was running in circles he wasn't sure

what he should do. David let out a sigh and placed his hand on Molly's knee. Then he slowly slid it up towards her thigh and stopped just shy of her pelvis. Molly placed her arm around David's shoulders and pulled herself closer to him.

"Took you long enough!" she whispered in his ear as she shifted closer. David's was now precariously close to her vagina. An ever so slight tingle shot down Molly's spine as the tension and temptation built. She kissed at first and then started sucking on David's earlobe. It wasn't long before Molly could feel something pressing into the side of her leg. Molly was pleasantly surprised but continued with her nibbling of David's ear. David softly started rubbing Molly's clitoris with his hand. Tingles raced up and down Molly's spine as David continued.

Finally Molly turned facing David and straddled his lap. As she sat there he just looked at her. The areolas of her breasts were still hidden by the water in the hot tub. Molly could just barely feel his nearly erect penis touching her clitoris. She just sat there looking into his eyes.

"So what are you thinking Babe?" she said still maintaining her position on his lap with her arms around his neck.

"Honestly I'm not thinking anything at all." He replied with a smile.

"Yeah right you are always thinking something. I know you to well to believe anything different." She teased.

"Well I am just waiting for one of your neighbors to catch us." David finally admitted.

"Well the only way that's going to happen is if they have a spy plane. My parent's had the whole back yard fenced with a nine foot tall privacy fence three years ago. After they were interrupted one night while they were in the hot tub. After that Mom refused to use it at all till Dad had the fence built." She paused looking like she was trying to remember something. "If I remember correctly she was the one that insisted it be a nine foot high fence because she didn't think the six foot high fence was tall enough." Molly finished.

David's mind was finally put to rest as he relaxed a little bit more. The warm water felt nice and Molly on his lap was even a better feeling. He attempted to slide himself forward slightly hoping to get closer to the prize he wanted.

"Oh don't be too eager." Molly teased as she pulled away. " We got all night for that." She added as she turned around so she was now facing away from him and sitting on his lap. She could feel his hard member pressing against her backside and she wondered what their first time was going to be like. It was going to be her first time

135

too but that didn't seem to scare her.

David reached around and grabbed both her breasts with his hands and pulled her into him as he softly fondled them beneath the water. Molly just leaned back into him enjoying the pleasure and the total privacy the two of them had. It was the one thing they both truly craved. Molly closed her eyes and just enjoyed the moment.

Molly's mind began to race as she thought about what the night was going to entail. She had masturbated a couple times, but she was sure actual sex was going to be much different. Then there was the size, he was definitely bigger than she was expecting, and definitely bigger than her fingers. Was it going to hurt she wondered. Pressed against her bare bottom it felt as if it were as big as a tree trunk. Her friend Janie had told her that her first time was painful. How painful she wondered but Janie never elaborated past that.

She had tried researching it on the internet. Once she was able to disable the filtering software her parents put on the computer she got a lot more than she bargained for. There was pictures, movies and articles galore. However nothing that really helped answer her questions. The pictures and movies were very confusing the expressions on the faces looked pained but the sounds indicated pleasure. Molly eventually just figured she would learn like

she always had through trial and error.

Molly was brought back to the present by David kissing her neck. David's hands then floated down to Molly's legs then found their way to their goal. David began rubbing between her legs again. As sensations traveled through her as she relaxed into David's body.

David continued rubbing Molly's clitoris as she just sat on his lap. He rubbed faster as her breathing increased. Molly was enjoying his touch as wave upon wave of pleasure crashed upon her body. Within moments Molly was achieving the first orgasm that wasn't delivered by herself. Molly collapsed backwards into David's chest as he continued to rub her.

After several minutes Molly stood up quickly, catching David by surprise. She hopped out of the hot tub and walked into the house without saying a word. David sat there just watching then after she disappeared from sight he saw her hand reemerge in the door motioning him to follow and then it disappeared again. David stood up as the water cascaded off of his body. He climbed out of the Hot tub and found his way to Molly's bedroom.

Molly was standing there next to her bed waiting for David. He crossed the room till he was next to Molly. Molly looked down and admired David's erect penis. Without saying a word she shoved David onto the bed and

jumped on top of him. David watched as she grabbed his member and guided it into herself as she lowed herself down onto it.

Molly was surprised by the size of it as she attempted to push it inside of herself. Slowly she slid down his enormous girth biting her lower lip. It was painful but it was pleasurable at the same time. It seemed like forever till she felt their pelvis's meet. Molly sat momentarily waiting for the pain to pass. She was surprised by the fact that the pain subsided quickly. David definitely felt good inside her, and he was definitely big. He was bigger than she was expecting, just sitting there she felt like she was going to tear apart.

David moved his hands up Molly's thighs and cupped her bare bottom. He slowly pulled her up and pulling himself out of her. Molly was instantly brought back to the present. Looking down at David she just moved his hands away and leaned forward placing her hands on his chest. She pulled herself up until David almost came out of her then reversed and slid back down. This time felt just as wonderful and was definitely easier.

Molly repeated the motion again and again, moving faster she noticed that they were both becoming really wet. She started dropping herself down harder on to David's large member. Each time she could swear he was going

further into her. Even further than he had at first. How is that even possible she thought to herself. She got lost in the pleasure and the pain of it. She came crashing down really hard and felt a crunch as their two bodies slammed together. Pain shot through her clitoris followed by a wave of pleasure as she exploded in a massive orgasm.

Molly almost collapsed onto David as her body quivered. David caught her and pulled her to his chest. Then without missing a beat he rolled Molly over so he was now on top of her and resumed delivering long hard thrusts deep into Molly. Grabbing ahold of her waist he delivered thrust after thrust. Molly arched her back as her body started to quiver. David continued his assault as she writhed beneath him. Molly threw her head back and started moaning, growing louder with every thrust.

David pulled up on her hips as he drove harder into Molly. His pace quickened as he felt himself getting closer to achieving his own orgasm. Molly was moaning louder as she reached her apex. In one strong thrust David exploded inside Molly. His intensity slowed but he continued driving himself into Molly as he continued to ejaculate inside her. After a couple more thrusts David came to a stop and came to a rest on top of Molly.

The pair laid there intertwined each barely moving. Molly's moaning was now replaced by heavy breathing.

David was also breathing hard, but just not as much as Molly had been. Molly was awash of emotions as she wrapped her arms around David trying to regain an ounce of composure.

"That…was…incredible…I mean wow." Molly finally stated breathlessly as she slid her hand up under her pillow. David just watched as she moved her hand around looking for something.

David smiled at her "Thank you" he replied as he shifted slightly causing himself to slide out from inside Molly.

Molly was surprised he came out so easily as it seemed like a feat to get him inside her to start with. She felt their combined juices draining out of her as her hand found what it was searching for. Molly pulled a pile of six to eight pages of paper out from under her pillow. She flashed a mischievous grin at David as she passed the papers to him.

"Think you might want to try some of these?" She inquired while David focused on the sheets of paper.

David thumbed through the pages each one had a different sexual position on it. Some of them David had seen before and a few were positions he hadn't or couldn't even imagine.

"I've been doing a little research." Molly injected.

"I can see that." David finally replied as he studied one

of the pages turning it around 360 degrees with a puzzled look on his face.

"Those are the only ones I feel brave enough to try. Well other than the standard ones." She added with a sheepish look on her face. "You think you might want to try one or two of them, or all of them?" Molly inquired.

"You seriously think you can do this one?" David asked as he looked at another page. Then showed it to Molly.

"I'm a gymnast, I think I am flexible enough. Besides I would like to try it too." Molly replied.

David placed the stack of pages on the nightstand. The top page had a diagram of the position they were about to attempt. The name at the top was The Venetian Oyster. David studied the picture for a few seconds then turned towards Molly.

"Are you sure?" He asked. Molly just nodded in agreement. David grabbed her legs and proceeded to lift them up off the bed and then pushed them towards Molly's chest. Moments later both Molly's feet were well above and behind her head. Molly adjusted slightly to get a little more comfortable. David just kneeled in front of her admiring the sight of Molly's contorted body, half astonished that she was even able to get into the position in the first place.

"Are you ready?" David inquired.

Molly let out a breath. "Yes just go easy on me ok." Molly replied.

David looked down at Molly's still extremely wet vagina tempting him. David positioned himself in front of her and placed the tip of his rock solid penis at the entry to her pleasure center. In one swift motion he buried himself inside her much more easily than he expected.

Molly's eyes shot open wide as David traveled deep inside her. The shear wave of immediate pleasure she experienced far outweighed the slight pain that accompanied it. David stared into Molly's eyes. They resembled small white saucers with emerald green marbles sitting in the center. Molly just nodded and David slowly started finding his rhythm gliding back and forth into her.

Molly couldn't describe the feeling even if she wanted to, it was unique and not like anything she had ever felt before. David was definitely traveling much deeper than he had before. It was almost a foreign feeling and yet extremely pleasurable. With every thrust wave after wave of enjoyment washed over her entire body.

David reached up and grabbed ahold of Molly's ankles with his hands and pushed backwards causing Molly's pelvis to project forward changing the angle of his penetration. In turn it also heightened the enjoyment for

the both of them. David's pace quickened and Molly felt herself having another orgasm. Before long Molly began to moan loudly again.

Molly's moaning was fueling David's actions. The louder she moaned the harder and faster David thrust into her. As David reached his apex prior to his climax he could feel himself slamming into her cervix as he erupted into a massive orgasm. Almost instantly after his Molly followed with another orgasm of her own.

David released his grip on Molly's ankles as he collapsed on the bed next to her. Molly gingerly extricated herself from the position she was in. Once she returned to a normal position she waited for her muscles to relax then cuddled up next to David. Molly could hear David's heart pounding as she laid her head on his chest.

"Are you enjoying yourself?" Molly finally broke the silence.

"Yes, very much. Are you?" he replied as his breathing returning to normal. "Give me a few moments and we can try something else." He added.

"Ok, I will need a couple moments too." she injected lying next to David.

Molly wasn't sure how much more her body could withstand, but she didn't know when they would have a chance like this again either. She was committed to getting

the most out of their time together as she could. Her legs were starting to stiffen slightly. While she was definitely quite flexible for gymnastics, the previous position required slightly more flexibility than even she thought it would.

The pair laid on the bed for almost half an hour not saying anything. Molly just kept her head on David's chest wishing she could stop the passage of time. She wanted this moment to last forever. She noticed David's member growing in her field of view. She figured David had found his second wind. Before she realized it David had flipped her over onto her stomach and pulled her knees up under her. Molly propped herself up on her arms as David grabbed her hips. Seconds later she felt him bury every inch of himself inside her.

David grabbed a hold of her hips hard and she enjoyed the very feel of his touch. Just like the time before it felt like he was able to travel deeper inside her than he had before. Molly enjoyed every feeling of pleasure she was sharing between David and herself.

David quickly and effortlessly found his rhythm and settled into a routine. Molly became instantly wet once David slid himself into her. Molly uttered a surprised tone as he thrust himself into her a little over zealously. David could feel himself hitting Molly's cervix as he continued

delivering his hard deep strokes. This was a feeling David was growing a custom too. This was also proving to be his favorite position.

David reached forward and placed his hand between Molly's shoulder blades and pushed down. Molly relented and lowered her upper body down onto the pillows. The change in the angle heightened the sensation she was experiencing. Her loud moans suddenly changed to screams as she buried her face into the pillow.

David pushed molly's knees apart slightly with his as he gripped her hips tightly. Molly's screaming was getting louder. The more vocal she got the more David got turned on. As he started to drive himself deeper and harder into Molly her screams grew louder. Moments later Molly's body began to tremble followed by a tremendous orgasm. Almost immediately afterwards David exploded in an orgasm of his own inside Molly's soaked vagina. David gripped a hold of Molly's hips tighter as he continued thrusting deep inside her.

Molly's screaming had subsided and was now replaced by her gasping for air. Her hips were sore and she could feel the fluids escaping and running down her legs. Each thrust David delivered felt deeper than the last and she wondered if he was going to break her in half. Finally her body could not take any further abuse and gave out.

Molly's body went limp and crashed to the bed. David didn't release the grip on her hips but followed her down to the bed then pushed every bit of himself deep inside her.

It was about ten minutes before either one of them even attempted to move. David was first as he felt himself slip out from inside Molly. Molly was lying in a small puddle of their combined juices. She wanted to move but her body was betraying her at every attempt. David rolled to the side then grabbed Molly and rolled her onto her back.

Molly tried to speak but couldn't emit any words from her mouth. David just looked at her then started running his hand up and down Molly's' naked body. David just watched as Molly's body reacted to his touch. As his hand glided over her breast he watched as the nipple became hard. He noticed goose bumps appear as his hand continued down across her stomach and down to her thigh. His hand crossed to her other thigh and glided back up her body to her other breast.

Molly laid there without uttering a single word. Every time she opened her mouth all that would come out was air. David looked down as his hand traveled its route over Molly's body. This time David's hand passed over then stopped atop Molly's bare shaven mound. It was definitely

different than his sister or his mother, but it was definitely something he liked. He pushed a finger into Molly's still wet hole and rubbed her clitoris at the same time. Molly's body reacted to his touch and after a moment Molly was finally able to speak.

"I appreciate you eagerness babe but I don't think I have enough left for another one." Molly said clearly sounding exhausted.

"That's fine, I understand." David replied as he kissed her forehead. David looked over at the clock and realized it was now well after 1230 in the morning.

"We should probably get some sleep." He added as he pulled the blankets up over themselves. Molly rolled onto her side as David snuggled up to her back. He reached up and cupped Molly's breast in his hand and relaxed. The last thing he heard was Molly softly snoring.

The sun light shined brightly through the windows of molly's bedroom. David rubbed his eyes as he reached out for Molly. But she was nowhere to be found in the bed. He rolled over to look at the clock to see it was 6:45 in the morning. David sat up and tried to get his bearings. To his surprise he found he was a little bit sore from the prior nights activities. Standing up he thought about putting on some clothes, but decided since they were alone it wasn't

really necessary.

David stepped into the hall from the bedroom and caught the smell of bacon and eggs. Quietly he walked towards the kitchen. He stopped when he saw Molly she was standing at the counter wearing nothing more than a small white t-shirt. He noticed that it was just long enough to just barely cover her little round butt.

David crossed the dining room quietly not making a noise and came up behind Molly. Molly was engrossed in an article in the morning newspaper. David grabbed her shoulders and pushed her over the counter top. Molly resisted at first but then accepted the positioning. As she bent over the counter David watched at the t-shirt slowly rise up exposing her beautiful creamy derriere. David knelt down behind her and shoved his face deep into her sweet vagina from behind. He drove his tongue deep inside her.

David worked his tongue back and forth inside her licking and driving it inside. Molly just laid across the counter making soft noises as David worked. Like the night before it was only a few minutes before Molly achieved an orgasm. The sweet nectar cascaded down onto David's tongue and into his mouth. After he finished his oral treatment he stood up and shoved his hard shaft into the now wet hole.

Molly let out an astonished and painful moan but then nothing more. David pushed himself deep inside her till he could go no further. He grabbed ahold of her hips and started slowly moving himself in and out of her. David slowly increased his speed as he settled into his rhythm. Molly just laid there enjoying the surprise activity. She was very sore, but just bit her lower lip and enjoyed every moment of it. She swore that David had grown in size and was now bigger than he had been the night before. After a few more particularly hard deep thrusts David and Molly both reached their climax at the same time.

"Well that is certainly a nice way to wake up." David said as he pulled Molly upright and against him. Still facing towards the kitchen Molly just wrapped her arms around David's neck.

"Yes it is. I could get use to this. Would you like some breakfast now?" Molly asked as she felt David's member soften and slip out from inside her.

"Yes it looks simply delicious." David said as he grabbed the two plates sitting on the counter and took them to the table. "But I think you are overdressed." David joked to Molly.

"So I am." Molly stated plainly and then quickly just pulled the t-shirt up over her head and dropped it on the floor next to the table. The pair sat at the table eating their

breakfast in silence. David just studied Molly's naked body or at least what he could see of it burning a mental image of her in his mind. He wanted to be able to remember this image as he was unsure of when he would be able to see her naked again.

Once they were finished eating David cleared the plates and rinsed them and put them into the dishwasher. Molly remained seated at the table just enjoying the time to relax. David returned to his chair and sat down. It was turned at a right angle to his place at the table and he just looked at Molly.

"Did everything taste OK? I know I'm not a great cook." Molly finally said breaking the quiet.

" You're a great cook." David answered. "Both dinner last night and breakfast tasted fantastic. Best I've ever had."

"Your sweet but I highly doubt that it was the best you've ever had." Molly smirked. "You think you want dessert now?" she asked.

"Sure." David replied not really sure what Molly was talking about. He just sat there and watched as Molly stood up and walked over stopping in front of him. She then kneeled down in front of David and grabbed his manhood in her hands and then took it into her mouth.

Molly's mouth traveled up and down his rod as it

proceeded to stiffen. She was sucking and flicking her tongue around it and then proceeded to take it all the way into her mouth. Molly continued the same movements precisely the same way repeatedly. After several minutes David could no longer maintain control and he grabbed the back of Molly's head and pushed her down hard on to himself as he burst into her mouth.

Molly was surprised by the sudden burst of cum in her mouth but she just swallowed a couple times and continued her previous motions. In about half the time of the first round David grabbed the back of her head again and pulled her down as he exploded a second time. This time it was considerably larger than the last. Again without hesitation Molly just swallowed it and continued. After a few seconds she realized David was no longer hard but was actually softening. As she stopped she looked up surprised to see David looking relaxed and physically spent.

David was impressed by Molly's surprising fellatio skills. As he watched her stand up.

"Oh no, did I break you?" Molly jokingly asked as she returned to her chair wiping her mouth.

"No, just need a moment to recover is all." David replied. Studying Molly's frame in the morning sunlight coming through the dining room blinds.

David and Molly eventually returned to her bed room and laid back down on the bed. As they cuddled up together on the bed they broke into casual conversation. Both of them were sore, Molly more so than him, not that either would admit it to the other.

Molly was the first to drift off to sleep. David followed shortly afterwards. After a couple hours Molly awoke not wanting to wake David she slowly extricated herself from David's grasp. Once free she stood up willing her sore muscles to work in spite of their painful protests.

Molly turned on the warm water and let the shower run. Slowly climbing in she let the water cascade over her body just enjoying the marginal relief it was giving her. She plunged her head under the water and quickly got lost in her thoughts.

CHAPTER 8

It was well after six in the evening when David got home. David was surprised to see that there wasn't a light on in the house as he drove up. The overcast day was quickly fading as the white clouds started to turn grey. It looked like it was just going to be another night at home alone. It really didn't bother him to spend time alone, it just really seemed to bother his family more. It was true he experienced bouts of depression, but what kid wouldn't having lost his Father and then having to be uprooted and moved away from the only home he ever knew. It just seemed to make his mom and sisters happy by having them around so he just put up with it, to placate them.

He grabbed his clothes out of the back seat of the car and headed for the front door. He looked up at the ominous looking dark clouds expecting them to release their rain at any moment. As he entered the house the downpour began. David threw his clothes in the hamper in his room. He headed into the kitchen to find something

to eat. He took a plate of left over chicken, and sat down at the table to enjoy the lackluster meal. As he was just putting the dishes from dinner in the dish washer he noticed the note sitting on the counter.

David –

Danni is working late and mom is stuck in L.A. till Monday. I'm over at Jenny's but you can call me if you need anything.

Love

Tina

The storm continued to rage outside causing the house to get darker to the point he had to relent and turn on a light. He sat down in the living room and turned on the TV. As was typical for a Sunday there was nothing on. After flipping through the channels three times David got up and decided to do something productive. He gathered his laundry and threw it in the wash. Then he gathered the rest of the families laundry and set it in the laundry room. Finally he returned to his room to play on the computer. As was the case with some nights David was having trouble keeping his mind on anyone thing for more than a

couple minutes. After getting killed for the twentieth time in his online game David just shut it off and went back into the living room and sat down on the couch.

For the first time in a long time he found that he was wishing either of his sisters were around just so he would have someone to talk to. He thought about calling Molly but her parents were definitely home by now and they would be monopolizing all her time. A fact that was confirmed by the fact that she hadn't showed up in chat on the computer when he was online. It was really the only way either of them could talk to each other when they weren't in school or studying at the library. Molly's over protective parents monitored her phone calls and David suspected her internet activity as well.

David resumed flipping through the channels on the TV till he stopped on something just to have background noise. The storm continued with fury outside as the thunder claps shook the house and the lightning strikes lit up the sky and the house bright as day. David considered calling his sister just to make sure she was alright but decided against it. She was at Jenny's and was as safe there as she was if she had been home. The last thing he wanted was for her to decide to come home and be out driving in the unrelenting storm.

A news alert came on the TV stating that the storm was

the worst storm the region had seen in over 50 years. And that anybody that didn't need to be out shouldn't be. If Possible the news man said everyone should shelter in place till morning.. There were reports of areas with flooding, and power and telephone lines down all across the city. Suddenly an extremely loud thunder clap exploded over the house shaking everything inside. It was so loud that David practically jumped out of his skin. Spinning around he looked out the window; instantly he saw a bolt of lightning pierce down from the sky and hit the transformer on the power pole outside by the street. The transformer exploded in a blinding flash as sparks sprayed in all directions. Then the entire house went dark as the power went out all throughout the neighborhood.

Everywhere David looked he saw the remnants of the blinding flash that burned itself into his vision. It would correct itself soon enough, but it was as if someone had just taken his picture with and old-time flash camera. With no power the house was as dark inside as it was outside. David turned and started heading towards the kitchen, and abruptly walked into the wall. Dumbfounded he figured it was best to wait till his vision cleared some before he attempted to navigate the house any further. As he sat on the floor rubbing his newly sore nose he strained to decipher what each of the blobs were about the room.

After a few moments his vision slowly returned to normal and he was able to at least make out things well enough to move about the house without injuring himself further.

Thirty minutes later the thunder and lightning had subsided, but the downpour of rain had continued. Looking outside David could just barely make out the river of runoff that traveled down the driveway and into the street. He figured it had to be close to 10 o'clock .and he was starting to wonder where Danni was. It wasn't like her to be this late considering that the store closed at 7 pm on Sundays. David made his way to his room and laid down on the bed.

The darkened house took on an eerie feeling. With the intense storm outside showing no signs of relenting. He had no options but to wait it out. As the winds started to pick up and buffet the house. The combination of the wind and the rain hitting the house made noises that he was certain he had never heard before. It wasn't that it scared him, but it almost seemed that at any moment the house could give way and be blown over. As he laid on his back he let his mind wander. He was trying to avoid thinking about what could have happened to Danni.

Ever since the death of his father it was often easy to jump to a tragic accident that left some one severely injured or worse. Especially when someone in his family

did something out of routine. Danni being late and not calling was completely out of routine.

As the next round of lightning and thunder started he caught himself counting the minutes. He should just go to sleep but it would have been impossible at this point. He was a nervous wreck, and nothing was going to change that till Danni got home. The wind made a particularly strong gust and the house made a loud pop. Startled David jumped to his feet. Deciding it was better to be doing something or anything to keep his mind off the dread it was now focused on. David started to move about the house looking for a candle or a flashlight.

Suddenly something large hit the front door of the house. His thought was that the screen door had blown open, or off by the sound of it. He walked over to the door and peered out the window. Outside stood his sister Danni soaking wet fumbling to find her keys. David opened the door as the wind wrestled it from his grip and slammed it against the wall. Danni stumbled into the house as David pushed the door closed and locked it.

"Where the hell have you been?" David screamed. "You have any idea what I have been through tonight?" He continued not giving Danni a minute to respond. "I have been worried to death." David was breathing heavy by now and he could feel his face getting red.

Danni just stood there dripping wet from head to toe. She had never seen David this mad ever. She understood why he was upset but not why he was yelling at her. In his entire life he had never once raised his voice to her or Tina.

"I'm sorry David, I was on my way home when the storm started. A tree had fallen across the road so I had to detour around. I ended up getting lost in a part of town I had never been in before. It took longer than I expected till I got back to someplace I recognized." Danni stated. She could see David was starting to calm down some. "Then I hit a large puddle of standing water and my car died. So I had to walk home in that storm and stupid me didn't take a coat to work." She added.

David stood there staring at Danni in the darkness of the house. In a moment he went from mad to concerned as he realized she was completely water logged. Her dark brown curly hair was wet and windblown into a mess that would take an hour to untangle. Danni almost seemed like she was in a state of shock. Then David saw her break down and start to cry. Almost instantly his fear changed to concern as he stepped over and wrapped his arms around his sister.

Touching his lips to her forehead he realized just how cold she was. Soon David's clothes were just as wet as

Danni's as he held her close trying to warm her up. Danni started to shake as David started to realize that she was at the beginning stages of hypothermia.

"Danni we got to get you out of these wet clothes and warm you up." He exclaimed. Danni just nodded then crumpled into her brother's arms. David half carried half walked Danni to her room. Even with the power still out his eyes had adjusted to a point he could see surprisingly well.

Danni turned and staggered into her room as David stopped to grab a towel from the linen closet. Walking into the room he found Danni sitting on the floor in the middle of the room removing her soaked canvas shoes. David kneeled down and wrapped the towel around her shoulders and started drying her hair. After a few moments her hair was damp and the towel was almost soaked.

He helped Danni get to her feet and then focused on getting her out of her still sopping wet clothes. Danni had chosen to wear her white linen pants and a white button up three quarter sleeve shirt. Not the wisest choice David thought as the rain had essentially made them invisible. David removed her pants and then started unbuttoning her shirt. Once he got her shirt off he unhooked her sheer white underwire bra and placed it on the pile of wet clothes on the floor. He then helped Danni dry off and lie

down in bed, covering her up with a blanket.

He took her wet clothes and the towel to the laundry room and set them in the basket. Luckily the storms intensity had lessened some and the house wasn't creaking quite as much. With the power out though they wouldn't have any heat till it was restored. While it usually wouldn't be a problem the temperature had dropped considerably outside and as a result the temperature in the house had dropped as well.. David noticed that his t-shirt was soaking wet and added it to the pile of clothes in the basket.

David stopped to check on Danni on his way back to his room and despite being under several blankets she was still shivering quite violently. He decided that the only option to get her warmed up was going to be to share body heat. He stepped over to her bed and lifted the covers and climbed in next to his shaking sister. She was laying on her side with her back to him so he reached around her waist and pulled her against his chest. The skin on her back was so cold it shocked him. He could feel that her abdomen was just as cold as her back.

It seemed like it took an hour before Danni finally stopped shivering. While the storm continued its mercilessness intensity battering the house with rain the two of them laid there in complete silence. David reached down and put his hand on her thigh. It was still cold but

not quite as much as it had been earlier. David climbed from the bed and walked to the kitchen to get something to drink. Looking at the thermometer in the dining room he saw it was about forty five degrees in the house.

Grabbing a small bottle of orange juice from the refrigerator he drank it down fast and threw it away. Quickly heading back to the room he climbed back into bed with his sister scooting up close to her this time in an attempt to warm himself up as well. He rested his hand on her hip and felt the band of the G-string panties she was wearing. Danni reached down and grabbed David's hand and pulled it over to rest on her stomach.

"I know what you're thinking but that's not happening tonight. Besides it is too damn cold." Danni stated.

"I didn't' think you were awake." David replied as he pressed himself up tighter against his sister. "And I wasn't thinking anything. Just making sure you were getting warmed up. You were really cold there for a while." Danni rolled on to her back and looked David in the eyes.

"You do know Tina talks in her sleep right?" She inquired as she read the look of surprise on David's face. "Yes, I know and don't worry I am not saying anything to anyone." She added as she rolled back onto her side. Now get over here and warm me back up." She said pulling David up against her back.

David laid there dumbfounded. What did she know? Tina? His Mother? Everything? He was confused and any attempt at getting any sleep was now going to be impossible. David just laid his head down on the pillow and tried to put it all out of his mind. A few moments later Danni grabbed David's arm again pulling it up across her chest placing his hand over her bare breast. Resisting the urge to squeeze it David eventually drifted off to sleep.

The sun pierced into the room exceedingly bright the following morning. David awoke in the same position he fell asleep in hours earlier his chest still pressed up against his sisters back and his left hand on Danni's breast. Danni was still asleep so David carefully extricated himself from her grasp and exited the bed. Before pulling the covers up he made a mental note of the sight of her bare g-stringed bottom and then left the room. The clock in his room was blinking 12:00 telling him that the power had finally come back on.

Looking out the window he saw a a couple of utility workers working on the power pole that had been hit last night. He turned on the news and wasn't surprised to see the images of the storms destruction, let alone the notice that all area schools were closed for the day and that some areas were still without power. David was watching the news when Danni walked up. She was wearing a t-shirt and

a pair of red yoga pants her typical weekend attire when she didn't have to work.

"No school huh? Well doesn't surprise me that was one heck of a storm last night." She said as she sat down on the couch next to David.

"Yeah it was quite a wild one. Thought it was going to blow the house down a couple times." David said. "Why did you walk home? Why didn't you just stay with your car? He questioned.

"Well while I was driving home and I hit the huge puddle causing the car die. I tried several times to start it but it just wouldn't do anything. I didn't think I was that far from home and that it wouldn't take me that long to walk home but the wind and rain made it difficult." Danni paused and let out a heavy sigh. "The wind besides being cold and blowing the rain around was so strong it knocked me over a few times. There was tree branches and debris everywhere. I fell a few times and twisted my ankle too. It just figures too that it would be the one night I choose not to take a coat with me." Danni finished. David could see a little tear in his sisters eye. Instinctively he put his arm around her and pulled her close. Almost instantly she threw her arms around David and broke down crying.

"You know how hard it is trying to handle all this?" She muttered threw her tears. "Dad's gone, Mom works so

hard and I am left to try and take care of you and Tina. Now my car is broke down and I don't know what I'm going to do." She added. David's shoulder was now soaked with tears but he just let Danni have her breakdown. After about five minutes of having a good hard cry Danni finally finished.

"Why don't you lay down and get some more sleep I will go look at your car." David offered as he stood up and helped Danni back to her room. Once she was back in bed David changed into jeans and a shirt and grabbed his cell phone. He fished Danni's car keys out of her purse and headed out the door. As he walked up the road he called Tina on the phone.

Tina talked about the storm and Danni. She said that the storm was worse at Jenny's house and she wouldn't be able to get home till around dinner. David told her not to worry everything was fine and he was going to find Danni's car as they talked.

David turned the corner and saw Danni's red Malibu sitting on the side of the road. It was only about three or four miles from the house. A little farther than he wanted to push it if he had to, but he hoped it wouldn't come to that. David opened the door and slid into the seat. Placing the key in the ignition he turned it and got nothing. No lights, no radio, not even a click from the starter.

"That's not a good sign." He said to himself as he reached for the hood release. He gave it a pull and the hood popped up easily. Getting out of the car he proceeded to raise the hood. He looked around the engine compartment looking for anything that might give him a clue as to what might be wrong. While he didn't know a lost about cars he knew some of the basics. I wish I knew as much about cars as I do about calculus. He thought as he checked the spark plug wires. He went back and turned the ignition again still nothing happened.

Frustrated David returned to poking around the engine compartment. Finally he noticed that the battery terminal connectors were not connected. Figuring they were loose and Danni hitting the pot hole must have been just enough to jar them off. Placing the connector on the positive terminal he twisted the nut as tight as he could with his bare hands.   Then when he attached the negative connector to terminal it caused a slight spark telling him there was at least some juice in the battery. Climbing back in the car he was rewarded when the engine started immediately.

Pulling into the driveway David parked Danni's car. And proceeded into the house. David kicked off his shoes and took a seat at his computer. As it powered up his phone started ringing. His mother was calling to let them

know she would be home in the evening since all flights into town were delayed till 4:00 PM. David told her everything was fine at home and he would see her when she got home.

Hanging up the phone he noticed that the internet was down so he just shut the computer down. Grabbing his phone he sent a quick text message to Molly saying he was fine and hoped she was too and that he would see her at school tomorrow. It was only 9:10 in the morning so he decided to jump in the shower. After the shower he decided to make breakfast his sister. After preparing a plate for himself and one of Danni he carried them to her room. Danni was still sleeping when he entered so he gently woke her up.

"What do you want now?" she groggily protested as she turned over.

"I made you breakfast and I brought your car home. No need to thank me." David said sarcastically.

Danni sat up taking the plate from him as David sat on the side of the bed.

"Really its fixed? What was wrong?" Danni quizzed as she took a bite of her scrambled eggs.

"Well the battery became disconnected. I suppose you were able to drive just on alternator power till you hit the puddle and it caused the alternator to short out. Which is

why it died." David took a bite of his eggs. "I'll tighten the battery connections later for you. The alternator should be fine." He added.

"Thank you so much." Danni exclaimed throwing her arms around her brothers neck almost knocking her plate on the floor. "I thought it was broken worse than that."

"Thanks for taking care of me last night." She stated as her mood became somber. "I don't know what would have happened to me without your help." She continued.

"It's ok sis we all take care of each other, that's what family does. Besides you were pretty hypothermic. If you hadn't got home when you did it could have been worse." David commented as he took another bite of his breakfast.

"Yeah well I'm sure you didn't mind undressing me either" she said smirking.

"Oh you remember that huh… at least I left your panties on!" David countered. As he stuffed another bite in his mouth.

"Yeah I remembered that! And I know you enjoyed it." She continued unable to resist teasing him further. "But I guess it's all fair though. After all I did see what you got too… even if it was by accident." She added not ready to let him off the hook just yet.

David quickly finished what was left on his plate hoping that would end the current topic of discussion.

"Did you have any plans for today? Its looks like they are trying to get things cleaned up but there is still a lot of trees and stuff down." He asked hoping to change the conversation.

"Not really I figured I would just stay home with you. since we would normally be in school right now had it not been canceled." She offered as she finished up what remained of her breakfast. "Since you cooked I'll do the dishes." Danni said as she jumped up and grabbing David's plate. Then she bent over to grab a dirty glass that was sitting on the corner of the night stand across the room. David just watched her. Her yoga pants were so tight it was making her ass look extremely nice. And her shirt was also hanging down just enough that he could see that she was not wearing a bra.

Danni could just feel David's eyes watching her every move. She lingered a little longer than needed making sure he got a nice good look. Then she stood up and walked to the kitchen. David followed shortly after her, and sat down at the table in the dining room across from the kitchen. He watched Danni like an eagle following a field mouse. As she moved about the kitchen cleaning up the remnants of David's cooking.

"What's on your mind David? You are awfully quiet. Probably the quietest I've even known you to be." Danni

inquired.

"Just thinking." He stated. More accurately he was trying not to think about anything, yet was failing miserably. As he watched Danni in the kitchen he was reminded about what she said last night. She says she knows, But what did she know exactly was the real question. He had to find out what she knew but had to be careful not to expose anything she didn't know.

"So Tina really talks in her sleep?" David asked despite his better judgement screaming at him to leave it alone. Danni just smiled to herself, David had taken the bait and she was going to reel him in and display him like a prize fish.

"Oh yeah, she is a real blabber mouth. She talks almost from the moment she falls asleep to the moment she wakes up." For the better part of the last few months it seemed Tina had been reliving her fun time as she called it every night. The first few times she mumbled so Danni couldn't make out any details and then one night she let a few bits spill. The next night a few more details spilled out. After a little more than a month Danni had pieced together the whole thing but still had no idea who Tina had slept with. Then one night while Tina was talking in her sleep Danni asked her directly who she had been with. To say she was shocked when Tina replied was an

understatement. Danni unconsciously asked our brother? To which Tina affirmed the question and then continued sleeping.

"But you know its ok. Not like it hasn't happened before." Danni added waiting to see what David was going to admit to.

"Well I mean she does have a vivid imagination." He stated hoping to deflect her assumptions.

"Yes she does but her story is the same every time doesn't vary one bit." She added as she wiped the counters down. "All I'm saying is that if what she said did happen it's not the end of the world." She still had her back to David as she bent over a little more so he could get a real good look at her round back end. After all she could tell he was intently watching her, she could just feel it. "Obviously it was a very memorable experience for her." She was taunting him now. As she emphasized the words very memorable.

"I don't suppose she said who she had this memorable time with though." David asked hoping he wouldn't get the answer he knew was undoubtedly coming.

Danni finished wiping the counter and tossed the dish rag onto the faucet as she straightened up. "Oh I think you know who she said." She spoke as she slowly turned around. "She said it was you." Looking David in the eyes

she watched as his eyes widened in surprise.

"She…uh… well… she's is wrong you must have heard her wrong." David stammered as Danni walked over to where he was sitting.

"No I heard her correctly." Danni said now standing right in front of David. "And I think I will take her up on one other thing she suggested to me too." She offered.

David was looking for an escape route but Danni was standing so close that there was nowhere for him to run. "Oh and what was that?" he quizzed.

"That I should try you out for myself." Danni finally spoke letting the tension finally disperse from the room. "What do you think?" She asked as she straddled David and sat down on his lap. David just sat looking bewildered as Danni proceeded to grab his hands and pull them up under her t-shirt, placing them on her bare breasts. "As I'm sure you are aware they are much bigger than Tina's." she smirked.

David started rubbing his sister. She definitely had larger breasts than his sister. Actually they were the biggest he had ever touched. Even more surprising was that both of her nipples were pierced with little rings. Danni threw her head back as she enjoyed his touch. After a couple minutes she grabbed one of his hands as she stood up.

"Of course I have a few other surprises that she

doesn't." She said as she slid David's hand past the waistband of her pants. David was surprised that she wasn't wearing any panties, but was even more astonished that as his hand traveled further she was completely shaved and then he felt something metal. Danni watched the inquisitive look cross David's face as he found her piercing and the little ring that sat there.

"Let me show you something." She said as she pulled David to his feet and unfastened his jeans. Once they were off she pushed him back down in the chair and pulled his shirt off over his head. "You can look but no touching." She said playfully standing in front of him.

David just nodded in agreement as he watched Danni take off her shirt and then peel the yoga pants off. As David's eyes scanned his naked sisters body from top to bottom and then back up again several times. He noticed that he was already hard as a rock. Danni had noticed this as well as she straddled him again and dropped herself down on top of his well-endowed member. David was surprised as he entered her with no problems and she in turn took all of him in one hard thrust.

Danni leaned back placing her hands on his knees and then started moving up and down traveling the full length of his penis with each movement. He was mesmerized watching her enormous breasts bounce as she rode him. In

a few short moments David felt his sister explode in an orgasm as she continued moving faster and falling down harder on his thick shaft. In quick succession she had three more orgasms.

She then stood up turned around and repositioned herself with her back to David. Then just as before she took him inside her and continued riding him. After a couple more minutes Danni threw her head back as she again had three more orgasms. David was trying to hold back but finally relented and had a large orgasm himself.

"It is about damn time." Danni said through heavy breath. "I thought you were never gonna cum." She added as she continued bouncing along on his slightly softened member. "I hope you don't think your done yet though? I have got a lot more to show you, and I don't want to waste this opportunity. Oh and you can now touch me." Danni asserted as she continued her bouncing.

David reached around and grabbed her bouncing breasts and squeezed them. "I always knew you were a boob man." She uttered.

"Yeah I do like boobs… But I really love your ass too." David stated as he slapped her round bottom.

"Come on I know you can hit harder than that." She laughed. As she felt him slap her ass again.

David slid his hand around to her front and found the

ring he felt earlier. As she continued bouncing up and down on his cock he started rubbing it and flipping it back and forth. Danni's eyes almost rolled back into her head as she exploded into and enormous orgasm.

"Damn how did you know about that trick I thought I would have to show you." She gasped as she came to a stop. David didn't utter a word but just pinched the ring and pulled on it. As it slipped from his fingers and snapped back Danni leaned her head back over his shoulder.

"You keep doing that and I'm gonna cum again." She whispered into his ear. "But if we keep doing this out here we are gonna have a bigger mess to clean up than just our clothes." Danni stated as she stood up. David watched her walk back towards her room. "Well come on I'm not finished with you yet." She said devilishly looking at him over her shoulder.

David caught up to her just as she turned into her room. Grabbing her he pushed her up against the wall and entered her wet hole from behind. As David started to punish her from behind Danni started to moan loudly after about five minutes they both reached climax at the same time. Without warning David pulled himself out and turned Danni around. Pressing her back against the wall he proceeded to enter her from the front this time and

resumed his hard thrusts.

After several more minutes Danni had another orgasm. David pulled himself out as she slid down the wall trying to catch her breath. As Danni sat there panting David just watched. her heaving chest. Danni was slowly regaining her breath as she stared at David's cock right in front of her face.

Grabbing her head he stuffed the full length of himself into her mouth. Danni gagged for a second then adjusted so she could take him completely, surprising David in the process. In a matter of moments she was swallowing the fruits of his labor.

She then stood up and once she had her legs under her she walked over to her bed and collapsed a top of it. David walked over to the bed with a half crazed look in his eyes. Danni knew David was enjoying this but she secretly wondered if she had bit off more than she could chew. While Danni was no stranger to long hard love making sessions this was not what she expected. So far David was even putting her boyfriend Jarred to shame. David turned Danni so her head was hanging off the edge of the bed and then watched as she willingly took him into her mouth again. After a few moments David bent over and started licking his sisters button and flicking the ring back and forth.

Moments later they both exploded in each other's mouths. David then grabbed Danni and put her on her hands and knees. As she got into position he spanked her round butt several times. He admired her ass as it began to turn red. Danni didn't utter one complaint as she let David due as he pleased. As he positioned himself to enter he grabbed her hips finding a familiar hand hold. Without warning he slammed his slick cock deep inside his waiting sister.

Danni's back arched almost instantly as her head shot back and she let out a loud scream. She felt as if David had just split her in half as he hit her cervix. As he pulled out she bit her lip as she readied herself for the next assault. Almost instantly he was delivering long hard thrusts each one hitting the same spot repeatedly. Eventually she reached her point and had one of the largest orgasms of her life. David continued for several more minutes until he had a massive orgasm of his own.

Danni collapsed and rolled onto her back as their fluids drained from her body. David collapsed beside her as he waited for his breathing to return to normal.

"Well that was definitely worth the experience." Danni finally said once she could mutter any kind of response.

"Yes it was." David agreed as he reached over and grabbed her hand. "I hope I didn't hurt you? I know I can

get carried away sometimes." He continued.

"No, I am fine but damn you have some serious staying power." Danni offered as her breathing returned to normal. "You want to get our clothes from the dining room I don't think I can walk."

David got up and walked out of the room as Danni turned to sit on the side of the bed. David returned with both their clothes and dropped them on Tina's bed then knelt down in front of Danni. He took her breast into his mouth and started to lick and suck on it. He felt her nipple harden in his mouth as he continued. He grabbed the ring with his teeth and pulled back stretching the nipple as far as he could then letting it snap back into shape. After several minutes he stopped and helped his sister to her feet and led her to the shower.

Once in the shower Danni assumed they were finished as David let her stand under the shower spray while he lathered her body up with the soap. She had to admit to herself that she was unprepared for the events that had transpired. David was exceptionally larger than she was expecting even putting her boyfriend Jarred to shame.

She got lost in her thoughts as she let David wash her entire body. Once he had finished washing her for the fourth time. They traded places under the shower head.

"I'm sorry I got a little carried away Danni." He finally

said. A little? she thought to herself.

"That's ok David… I actually enjoyed it a lot more than you realize. I kinda like rough sex." She admitted as she lathered him up. Reaching around his waist she could feel he was still hard as she cleaned him.

David turned to face his sister as the soap rinsed off his back. Then he took the bar of soap from her hand and placed it on the shelf. David grabbed his sister and spun her around pressing her up against the tile wall of the shower. The tile was cold against her bare chest as she felt David fill her up again from behind. One thing she knew for sure was that he knew how to get her body to react. His very touch was enough to make her body quiver. As she quickly reached another orgasm she relented to accept her fate. With David showing no signs of stopping anytime soon. She knew she was in for another session. Whether her body could handle it or not was another matter entirely.

CHAPTER 9

April was unusually warm for this time of year. As was the routine high school seniors were ordering caps and gowns and dreaming of graduation. Danni was no different as she stood looking at her reflection in the mirror wearing the maroon cap and gown. "I think this is the right size." She told the sales lady as she turned around. After removing them she laid them on the small counter by the mirror and joined the sales woman at the counter. "It's $45 correct?" she asked as she pulled her wallet from her purse and opened it.

"Yes, and it will arrive at your house about two weeks before graduation." She said as she rang up the sale. Danni took her receipt and left the store and headed down the block.

Danni walked past the Victoria Secret store, as she glanced at the panties in the window her thoughts were taken to the experience she shared with her brother. Many times she had wanted to tell Tina and compare notes.

However that would have just seemed like gloating. Besides it was an experience that was just between the two of them. She had often replayed the events in her mind. A couple of times she even considered having another go just for fun. That however would never happen and she knew that, It was just a onetime thing. Now all she has is the memories. But what wonderful memories they were.

Tina was beyond bored as she sat in her car in front of the library. David was supposed to be done about an hour ago what on earth is taking him so long. She wondered as she started fidgeting with her key chain for the hundredth time.

Moments later she saw David appear from the side of the building and head straight for her car.

"Sorry, I know that took longer than expected." He said as he slid into the front seat of the blue Volkswagen. "Mrs. Harrington wouldn't let anyone leave till time had expired."

"I don't even know why you bothered to take them again you took them at the first of the year and scored 1495." Tina said as they left the parking lot. "There isn't a school in the country that is gonna deny you with that score."

David knew she was right but it also kind of made him mad that Tina had scored 1530 on her SAT's.

"Of course it's still not as good as my score." She threw in knowing it would get under David's skin.

"Yeah rub it in sis. I'll get even later." He smirked then just looked out the window. "Hey pull into Applebee's it's my treat." David offered.

Tina sat at the table just looking at her brother. What had seemed like a good idea for a little fun had backfired. Whether she realized it at the time or not she had become forever linked to her brother. True they were just as close now as they had ever been maybe even closer if that was possible. Nothing had really changed between them at least not for him anyway. The thing was David had Molly and that was the way it was supposed to be.

But for her things were different. She wanted David to forever be with her. To a point he always would be he was after all her brother. But the heart wants what the heart wants she tells herself. For David his heart wants Molly and as such she hast to figure out how to make her heart let go. David will always be her brother and she will always love him. She knows however that she will never have him like she wishes she could.

Molly sat on the table in the Doctor's office. Come on how long does it take to read some stupid tests, she thought to herself. Her mother just sat in the chair nervously turning pages in a magazine she was clearly not even reading. She looked down at the large bruise on her lower leg. It was dark and wasn't healing like it should have. She was use to bruises it came with the gymnast life but this one was different. If had just appeared overnight and has not healed or even gotten smaller. She knew that was not normal but she tried to not focus on it till she had some real answers.

Finally the knock she was both eagerly waiting for and dreading came at the door. As the door slowly opened she saw the doctor come in holding a rather thick looking folder. "Well we got some answers...some good... some bad." He said as he let the door close behind him.

Alyson sat on the couch drinking a cup of mint tea. She knew she was breaking her own rule about have anything to eat or drink while sitting on the living room furniture but she didn't much care. It was her house by the way. She thought it was eerily quiet though. It was strange not to have at least one of the kids home. She let out a long sigh and took another sip of her tea. She may as well get use to

the quiet she thought. After all Danni would be heading to College in the fall, and David and Tina would be following the year after.

Maybe she would get a dog, or maybe buy a smaller house. Maybe she would just pick one of the kids and move to whatever college town they chose. That was the idea she had kicked around the most. Especially since all three had currently chosen Universities in the same state. Danni had received a scholarship to USC and was planning on getting a degree in Marine Biology. Tina on the other hand had her sights set on Stanford, and David well he wanted to go to UC Davis because they had a great swimming and diving program. The fact that it was his father's alma mater and it had a good business program was a close second.

No matter what she chose her job was flexible enough to allow her to move anywhere. The question was really where did she want to go.

Alyson, Tina, David and Molly all sat in the auditorium at Danni's graduation. As she crossed the stage and got her diploma. Alyson couldn't contain her excitement anymore and let out a loud "You did it Girl" yell. The crowd applauded and the graduates continued to cross the stage.

Afterwards the five stood outside on the grass as parents and students took pictures and talked amongst themselves.

"This will be us next year." Molly said to David as she held onto his arm.

"Yeah, I know time really flies doesn't it?" David asked as he watched his mom take picture after picture. "You know she is gonna point that thing this way sooner or later."

"Yeah I know it's ok I'm ready for it." She said as she laid her head on his shoulder.

"You feeling alright?" David asked.

"Yeah sure I'm just a little tired is all. Haven't been sleeping well the last few nights it's not a big deal." she tells him as she fights to hold back a yawn.

David let the matter go just as if on que his mother turns around to get a picture of the two of them.

After dinner David drove Molly home then returns home. His family sits around the living room talking and laughing. It's a fun time that hasn't happened in a very long time at least not since his father past away. Everyone is in high spirits. But like a dark omen something just isn't quite right.

Among his family everything is great. His Mom's job is going great and she is probably the happiest he has seen her in months. His sister Danni is excited to move on to

the next chapter in her life as college awaits with a whole new set of adventures. As for Tina and him they are fine too. They know it will be tough when Danni moves out and goes to college but they will weather that storm together like they always have.

Yes everything is going great but still something is wrong. What that something is not ready to reveal its self to David, at least not yet anyway.

David's mom jumps up. "We should have a toast." As she hurries to the kitchen a grabs a bottle of champagne that she had put in the back of the refrigerator a week earlier and grabs four glasses. She opens it and pours each of them a glass. They all drink it and converse till late into the evening.

David wakes up the next morning with intentions to find a part time summer job. As he gets out of the shower he hears his cell phone buzz. Looking at it he sees a message from Molly simply saying "We need to talk" then followed by another "Halo Restaurant 11:30 our table"

David finishes drying off and heads to his room to get dressed. The Halo Restaurant is more of a bistro than a restaurant. It has a secluded table in the back that is almost completely hidden from the rest of the restaurant. It was Their personal hiding spot a place where they could relax

and hide away from everybody. Some of his best conversations and memories with Molly were at that table.

David arrives at the restaurant fifteen minutes early to find to his surprise that Molly was already waiting for him. He walks up to the table, bends down and gives her a kiss on the cheek then slides into the chair sitting directly opposite her.

"Nice to see you. I thought you had some appointments today?" David asks as he takes a drink from the glass of water. Molly just sits almost stoic and David knows this is not a good sign.

"I do…I just had to…ugh…well" Molly stammers as she tries to find the words. David knows this is bad, the bad omen is here and he knows it is going to hurt. He hardens himself hoping it will soften the blow. Molly's eyes fill with tears as she tries to hold them back. But it is too late now.

"I haven't told you something because I don't know how to tell you." She starts as tears start rolling down her cheeks. David finds that place in the deepest part of his soul where he hides when the world is about to implode. It is the only place he feels safe. It is the place that he hid after his father died. It is the place that Molly managed to pull him out of. And he finds it strangely fitting that it is her that is about to put him back into that cell.

"Whatever it is we can work through it… together." he pauses "That is if you want too." He adds then waits silently for the death blow to come.

The tears start falling freely down Molly's face in the last month she has cried almost every day. She thinks that she should be all cried out by now. But alas every day she is able to cry a little more. "David I have cancer." She finally manages to speak. "It's in my bones in my leg" The doctors are going to have to remove my leg but they say they think they can get it all." She draws a big breath in. "My gymnastics and diving is over. And worst of all I won't be a whole person anymore." She sputters through more tears. "I wouldn't blame you if you wanted to not see me again." She finishes between sobs

David sat there stunned he didn't know what to say. What he did know is that he definitely didn't want to leave. "That's it?" He said after what seemed like an eternity to Molly. "You expect me to just get up and walk out of your life after all we have been through?" David was mad: more hurt really that Molly would even suggest such a thing. "I love you Molly and that means you are stuck with me whether you like it or not." David was barely keeping his anger in check. "I could care less if they have to take your leg if it means that they can save your life." He paused "But I will be damned if I'm gonna walk away. You want

me gone then you gotta tell me that to my face Molly. You got to make that choice. Not me. Because my choice is to stay right here." David took another drink from the glass of water as he watched Molly just sitting there shocked.

This was not what she expected. Not only that but this was the angriest she had ever seen David get. She was stunned, she was prepared for him to get up and leave. Part of her wanted him to get up and leave But no not David there he sits just staring back at her waiting for her to say something, anything.

"I...I...I love you too David." Were the only words that came from her mouth.

"Then we will meet this head on. Together." David said as he reached across the table taking Molly's hands.

CHAPTER 10

Fifteen Years Later

"Emily, Tabitha come on. Your gonna be late for school…again." David yells down the hall. Emily comes bounding around the corner her blonde hair in a ponytail. She gives her dad a kiss on the cheek and disappears out the door. Tabitha follows close behind her younger sister her long brown hair pulled up into a nice bun.

"Love you Dad." She says as she kisses him on the cheek and grabs the two lunch bags he is holding.

David follows her out the door watching her walk towards the van that takes the girls to school. "Don't forget I have to go out of town so you are…"

"Staying at Aunt Tina's tonight. I know Dad you only told us like a hundred times." She says as she pulls the car door closed behind her.

David watches the van drive off down the street and

around the corner. To say it had been hard since Molly passed away would be an understatement. But being a father gave him a reason to get out of bed every morning.

Molly's first surgery was successful. The doctors were able to get all the cancer and only needed to take her left leg from just below the knee. She quickly rebounded back and to David's surprise she was able to run even faster with the prosthetic leg than he could with two normal legs. He would often tease her about them secretly giving her a bionic leg. Because that was the only explanation for her to be even faster than before.

Molly and David were married their sophomore year of college. Molly had broken the news about him being a father as a graduation present two years later. Despite feeling that they were not ready to have a family. He couldn't have been happier when Tabitha was born. Three years later Emily came along and then they had everything they wanted. Now at 10 and 7 he is reminded of their mother every time looks at them.

Sometimes it's hard because he see so much of her in them and very little if any of himself. They both have her eyes, and her nose. Tabitha has her whit, and Emily has her sarcasm. But every day he gets to see his wife in the faces of his two daughters.

They had been talking of having a third child when

they learned that Molly's cancer had returned that was just three years ago. Despite the treatments and the chemo Molly lost her battle. She passed away on their anniversary in David's arms. Letting her go was the hardest thing he ever had to do. The second hardest was telling his two little girls that their mother had died.

David was a devastated man. It took a little time and help from his family to get him back on his feet again. His sister Tina had even moved into his basement for almost a year so she could help David with the girls. Danni who had also ended up settling in the San Jose area, also helped out when she could but her job kept her busy.

David's Mom relocated to San Francisco and was the reason David wasn't bankrupted with Molly's medical bills. She had without their knowledge taken out life insurance policies on each of them when the girls were born just to have a safety net. David was upset at first when she told him after Molly's death but he understood why she did it.

To say this was not how David's plan for his life would go was an understatement. His plan was to see the girls grow up and for him and Molly to grow old together. But life always has other plans.

Tina received a scholarship to Stanford where she studied Psychology. After she graduated she met Alex and

they were married a short time later. Then after what could only be called a rocky year and a half marriage they got divorced. She moved in with Danni for a short time before she decided she needed a change and quit her job and started selling real estate in San Jose. Seeing a good opportunity she bought a city block of homes with the intent to flip them and make quick money. She fell in love with one a decided to keep it. Then David and Molly wanted to buy the house three doors down from her. With the exception of college David and Tina had never been more than a few hundred feet away from each other for most of their lives. It was a trend that had continued David was a devistated into their adulthood.. Not that either of them seemed to mind.

Tina enjoys a quiet life helping David with the girls and selling real estate in the San Jose and San Francisco areas.

Danni graduated summa cum laude with a Phd in Marine Biology. She met and married Gunther while doing research on Sea Lions off the Oregon Coast. Gunther is from Germany and they have two very handsome twin boys. Danni, Gunther, Hunter and Hans live on the south side of San Jose. When she isn't doing field research she teaches Marine Biology classes at San Jose State College.

Alyson bought a small home in San Francisco where she continues to work in Insurance. She enjoys being close to her children and grandchildren. When Molly passed away she helped David as much as she could with the girls while David was dealing with losing his wife. Despite protests from her family she continues to look out for them as much as possible.

David turns to walk back inside the house as he notices his sister walking up holding a cup of coffee.

"Good Morning. They look more and more like their mother every day." She says as she takes a drink of her coffee.

"Yeah that's a good thing imagine if they looked like me." He jokes as he grabs the newspaper and walks into the house. "You sure you're ok with the girls this weekend? I can cancel or send Thomas to do the meeting." He says as she follows him inside and closes the door.

"I'll be fine, besides I love them and they love their Aunt Tina."

"Yeah, yeah, yeah everybody loves Tina" he says sarcastically.

"You go ahead and take your trip. You're the boss you have to do boss things once in a while." she takes another

drink. "Me and the girls will be just fine besides I have been taking care of you all my life and you turned out ok." She winks.

"Yeah I know but I just worry."

"Yeah, all you ever do is worry. It's what makes you a good father, It makes you a good man." She states

"I mean what happens if I have a heart attack or the plane crashes, or.."

"My god quit being such a drama queen...You are as fit as a horse you run 5 miles three times a week and you eat more vegetables in one week than I did all last year. If anything you're going to outlive all of us." She says slapping him in the back of the head.

"Besides mom has all of us insured to the hilt, you die I'm going to be rich and the girls won't have to worry about anything." She smiles as she finishes the last of her coffee. "After all you and Molly did decide you wanted me to raise them if something happened to the both of you."

"Ok well thanks for the pep talk I guess." David says as he grabs a cup of coffee and starts drinking it. "So what do I owe your wonderful pleasure this morning."

"I just wanted to make sure the girls got off to school and that I didn't need to drive them." She refills her cup with the remaining coffee from the pot and turns it off.

"You know I am quite capable of taking care of the

girls and myself." He says grabbing some papers and placing them in to his briefcase.

"Oh I know you are capable of taking care of yourself and the girls. If I didn't come over though how would I be able to give you a hard time, and you would start to think I didn't love you anymore. Besides without me you would have to learn how to tie a tie correctly. Come here." She says as she unties his tie and starts to retie it. Once tied she grabs a hold of the tie and pulls him in and gives him a kiss on the lips. "There now you look pretty." She jokes.

"Men are not supposed to be pretty." He replies sternly.

"Then why you wearing fingernail polish?" She asks smirking.

"I'm what? Oh the girls, well Emily wanted to play beauty parlor last night. I thought I got it all off. I guess I missed that one." He says grabbing the nail polish remover out of the bathroom cupboard.

"You know what you need is another male around the house. Maybe a baby boy." She suggests as she grabs the nail polish remover pads from him and starts rubbing the polish off his finger nails.

"We have had this conversation before. And I'm not ready to date yet. I don't know that I will ever be ready. Besides I don't think the girls would understand another

woman in the house." He says shaking his head.

"Ok I will let it go. There nice male masculine nails again. Honestly what would you do without me?" She asks as she puts the nail pads away.

"Probably move in with mom." He replies jokingly. "Have you had breakfast?"

"No, What do you want Corn Flakes or Raisin Bran?" She says opening the cupboard.

"Corn Flakes is fine with me." He says as he passes by her to grab the milk from the refrigerator. Passing back by again he slaps her on the behind with his free hand.

"What was that for?"

"It was in my way. Besides you never use to mind that."

"Yeah well you never use to mind that I was in your way either." she retorts.

They both sit at the table eating their cereal and talking about various topics. Once they are finished Tina grabs the bowls and places them in the dishwasher and starts it. As they hear a car horn blow in the background.

"Well that's my cab. You still able to pick me up Sunday afternoon at the airport?"

"Yeah I will be there. 4:30 right?" she asks as she follows him to the door.

"Yeah, anything else?" He asks as he turns to face her.

"Just one thing." She says as she grabs him and kisses him again this time giving him a kiss like she use to when they were younger.

"I'm Pregnant!"

ABOUT THE AUTHOR

Alistair McDonald is the pen name of a Scottish author
who often writes stories about alternate lifestyles and
taboo topics. He lives in Inverness with his wife Anne and
two terriers Simon and Tassy when he is not writing he
enjoys walking on the beach with his dogs and playing the
Bagpipes.

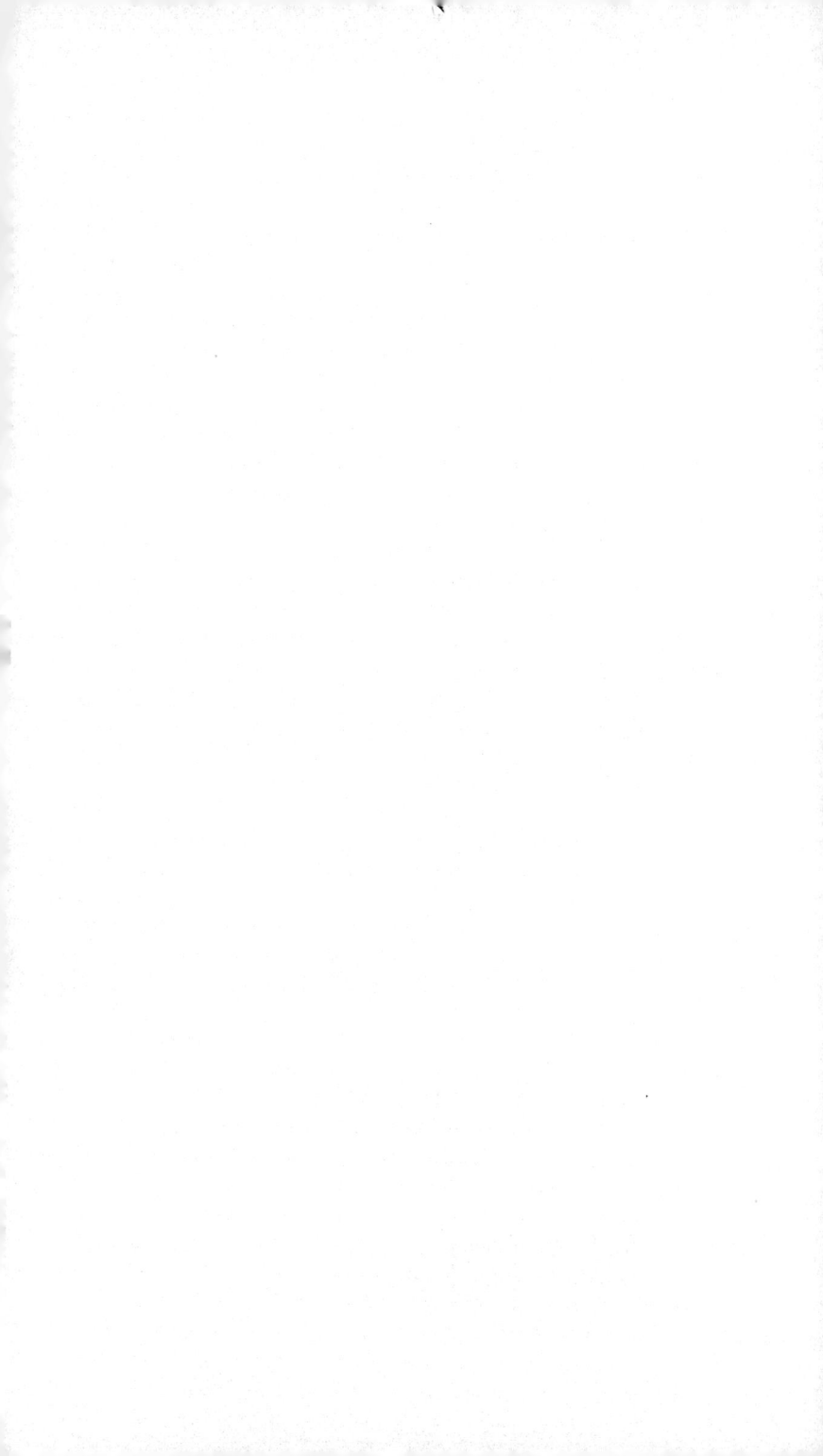

Printed in Great Britain
by Amazon

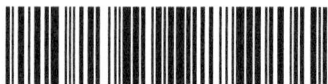